Dangerous

By

Mia Faye

Table of Contents

Copyright and Disclaimer *3*
Chapter 1 .... *4*
Chapter 2 .... *14*
Chapter 3 .... *24*
Chapter 4 .... *33*
Chapter 5 .... *42*
Chapter 6 .... *52*
Chapter 7 .... *61*
Chapter 8 .... *71*
Chapter 9 .... *80*
Chapter 10 .... *88*
Chapter 11 .... *97*
Chapter 12 .... *107*
Chapter 13 .... *116*
Chapter 14 .... *126*
Chapter 15 .... *136*
Chapter 16 .... *144*
Chapter 17 .... *154*
Chapter 18 .... *162*
Epilogue *169*

Copyright and Disclaimer

Copyright © 2023 by Mia Faye

In no way is it legal to reproduce, duplicate, or transmit any part of this document in either electronic means or in printed format. Recording of this publication is strictly prohibited and any storage of this document is not allowed unless with written permission from the publisher. All rights reserved.

This book is a work of fiction. Any resemblance to actual persons, living or dead, or actual events is entirely coincidental. Names, characters, businesses, organizations, places, events, and incidents are products of the author's imagination or are used fictitiously.

Chapter 1

ABBY

"No! Get your hands off my parents," Bailey screamed.

"I'll kill you," my father yelled at the police officer. *"I'll hunt you down and cut your heart out."*

"George, stop threatening him; it's just going to make it worse. Girls, you take care of yourselves. We'll be back for you. It's just a few days. We'll be back," my mother sobbed.

"I'll do whatever the hell I want and this son of a bitch better watch his back," my father continued.

"I love you, girls. I love you," our mother said as she was put into the backseat of the police car.

"I'll die without my mommy," Samantha cried as she ran toward the police car.

"Mommy ... Mommy ... Mommy ..."

I woke up, sitting bolt upright in bed as the dream settled into my mind. It wasn't the first time I had dreamed about that horrible day. It had been the moment when my sisters and I lost our parents forever.

No one ever thinks they can survive the loss of their parents. Luckily, most people never have to deal with it. But our parents made some pretty big mistakes, and they paid for them dearly, but so did we.

I remembered that day so vividly, even without dreams it was very clear in my mind. I held onto my sisters Bailey and Samantha as they both cried uncontrollably for our parents. They cried for hours and hours. When the social worker came to get us, I couldn't take it another minute and finally let the tears quietly roll down my cheeks as well. It wasn't the first time we had seen them taken away by the police. But it was the first time I had felt so much dread.

Mrs. Lynton was our social worker and, on that day, she appeared unusually solemn when she arrived. Her normally optimistic attitude was gone, and I didn't know why. Later, I would learn that she already knew we weren't going to get to see our parents again. She had been working with them, and they were on probation. But this arrest was their last chance, and the social worker knew that they were going away for a very long time.

"Girls, we have a foster home for all three of you, this time," she had said to us. "You won't be separated."

You would think that would have made me happy, but the truth was, I didn't care. My emotions were dulled to the situation, and I couldn't stand to be anywhere that I felt caged up. The Barristers were the nicest foster parents we had ever had in our ten years of back and forth between home and our parents. But it didn't matter to me. If I couldn't have my parents, I wanted to be on my own. I was seventeen years old, and there was nothing the Barristers could do to convince me I should stay in Wichita, Kansas another second.

When Mrs. Lynton came about a week after our placement to tell us that our parents would not be able to regain custody, this time, I lost it. I lost my teenage mind. The screaming started as an involuntary reaction to the hurt I felt inside. But then I couldn't stop myself; I didn't want to stop myself. When I finally ended up locked in my room, I knew I needed to leave. I had to get away from Bailey and Samantha and give them a chance to be happy. They were only 16 and 13 years old. They were still children, and they deserved to try to be happy.

It's funny to me that I thought of Bailey and Samantha as children but I thought of myself as an adult. I was only a year older than Bailey and certainly could have used the love and understanding of a caring adult. But my heart was in so much pain, I couldn't stay in that home another moment longer. I honestly thought I was doing what was best for my sisters. I believed that leaving them there was better than me staying there with them.

I was almost 18 when I ran away, so the state didn't look for me very hard. They figured I was more trouble than I was worth, and it was probably better that I had left instead of causing a bunch of trouble in the foster home. Kids in foster homes were often getting into fights and causing so much chaos that they had to be placed in special units that were run by the state. I felt like I would have ended up in one of those units if I had stayed there.

Our foster parents were kind, but with each nice comment they made toward me, I felt myself lashing out at them. They couldn't replace our parents, and no matter how nice they were to us, that would never change. It would never bring our parents back.

In retrospect, I was hurting and scared. I thought I was grown up enough to know better than the adults around me. I didn't. But I couldn't take back the past and the decisions I had made were what made me who I was in the end. They made me strong enough to deal with absolutely anything that came at me. I didn't need someone to take care of me, I could take care of myself.

Leaving my sisters was the hardest thing I'd ever done. But I tried to stay in touch, and now that Samantha had just turned 18, both my sisters were living on their own. Bailey had moved into our old family home when she turned 18 with the help of a local church group, and Samantha had just recently moved in with her. It was perfect for them, but I knew they were having a hard time paying the bills. Plus, they had received some notices about owing back taxes as well. I had to make more money so I could help them.

It had been four years since I arrived in New York City with dreams of acting on Broadway. As I lay in the bed of a man I didn't know, in an apartment I had never been in before, I certainly wasn't living the dream that I'd had for myself. But whoever got their dreams when they wanted them? I didn't expect things to come easily to me, and I was more than willing to work for the life I wanted.

My life wasn't horrible, though. George was a guy I had met while out at a club with Isabella. He was kind and seemed rather lonely. We talked and danced and had a great night together. When he invited me back to his place, I knew I would say yes. The nice guys were the best ones to spend time with.

"Good morning beautiful," George said as his naked body rolled over and he kissed my hand.

He had been naked in the hope that I would want to do more than sleep next to him in the bed. But he obviously didn't know that I was using him for his warm and comfortable apartment. He was a nice guy, and someday I was sure that he would find a decent girl; it just wasn't going to be me.

Everything about George repulsed me. His pale skin, the zits on his face, they all made me absolutely sick to my stomach. But coming home with him hadn't been about having sex or being attracted to the guy. I chose George because he was harmless. He was the kind of guy who probably didn't bring that many women home with him, and he was the sort of guy who wouldn't force the issue if I didn't sleep with him. In my world, nice guys were exactly who I was looking for. Not because I wanted to date them, but because I needed a place to sleep.

"Morning," I said as I put my actress skills to work and flashed him a brilliant smile.

Men liked it when you smiled in the morning; I had learned that over the years. It was hard to find a man to date in New York City. Most of them were so caught up in their jobs that they didn't want to take the time to get to know someone. But it wasn't hard to find a guy to go home with when I needed to; the unattached nature of a one-night stand was easier on a man's brain.

It typically started as one night. But then I was sweet to them, sweeter than any girlfriend they had ever had before. We laughed, made breakfast together, and I left nonchalantly without a care in the world. But I always got their number and always stayed in touch. For weeks, I would flirt and build them up, in the hopes of finding one I could stand to live with for a little bit.

Sometimes, I came across a man that I liked enough to stay with for a week, and sooner or later I would give in and have sex with him. But typically, I didn't stay long enough to ever have any real emotions about a guy.

"How are you feeling?" George asked me.

His hand traced up and down my arm as he looked at me with genuine concern. I had pretended to be sick in the middle of our passion the previous evening. It was a ploy to keep me from sleeping with him, and it had worked.

I did have to suffer through his naked, hairy body lying next to me all night long, but that was a small price to pay for a comfortable bed in the middle of winter. I had slept in much worse conditions and was grateful to have made a connection with George.

"I'm still a bit fuzzy," I said as I smiled at him and held his hand. "Maybe some food would help?"

I was starving, not having eaten much at all in the last couple of days. Only a few scraps of food from the restaurant I worked at and some drinks that George had purchased for me the night before. It wasn't unusual for me to go without eating, but I never got used to it. When your body was hungry, there wasn't much else you could do but find some food and give yourself the nourishment you needed.

Mostly, I held his hand to prevent him from trying to slide it anywhere that I didn't want it to go. But it was a nice touch of intimacy as well. There was a balance of intimacy that was needed to hook a guy, and I wanted that balance not to include sex.

Sure, I sometimes slept with a guy when he was extremely handsome and someone I wanted to date in the long run. But those guys were few and far between. I had expertly come up with a plan of seduction that was working for me and it didn't involve sex at all, just the promise of sex in the future ... when I felt better.

Men were predictable creatures, and if you coddled them and promised them your body, they would almost always give me exactly what I wanted. I wanted to hate my life, but I actually really liked the attention from men. The power that came with seducing them was exhilarating.

"Would it help if I made us some breakfast? Or would you prefer to go out and grab something?" George asked as he got out of bed.

His cock was fully erect, and I tried not to look directly at it as he stood over the bed. He wanted me to see him. He wanted me to see how much his body wanted to be inside of mine, but I didn't care. I was about to eat breakfast and then leave. I'd put George in my phone book as someone I could call again down the road when I needed an emergency place to stay for the evening.

"Oh, yes. Let's eat here," I said as I turned my back to George and got out of bed. "I'm so hungry, I don't think I will even make it to a restaurant."

I took an exceptionally long time stretching and pulling my hair into a ponytail hoping that he would finally go put some clothing on before breakfast. But I didn't say a thing about him exposing himself to me. There was no need to say anything. I wasn't trying to get George to be someone that he wasn't. I didn't really care all that much if he exposed himself to me. All I cared about was the fact of having slept ten solid hours in a nice warm bed.

The situation was unique for him, I was pretty sure. Typically when a guy had convinced a girl to come home with him, there was no doubt that he was going to get lucky. But poor George didn't know that I had no intention of sleeping with him. I simply wanted to sleep.

As we sat at his dining room table, I took in the rather large New York City apartment that he had. George had said he was a business owner, but I couldn't remember what he did. His apartment was by far the biggest I had been in for at least the last few months. In New York, that was saying a lot since most apartments were smaller than a typical living room from where I was from.

"Your eyes are amazingly blue and beautiful," George said, staring at me while we ate our scrambled eggs.

"Thank you."

"And your hair, it's like the perfect shade of brown, and so soft," he said as he reached up and ran his fingers through my hair.

I knew exactly where he was trying to lead things, and I needed to put a stop to it if I wanted to get to work on time. My day job, as a waitress, was essential to meeting high-quality guys, and I couldn't lose it. The last two real boyfriends in my life I had met while waitressing. I needed to be on time to that job.

"Thanks so much for last night George. You were such a gentleman. Not too many guys are out there like you. I truly appreciate your sweet and genuine caring about my wellbeing."

"Oh, you're welcome," he said, pulling his hand away from my hair. "I always make sure to treat women with the utmost respect."

It was a classic move; tell a guy he was a gentleman, and he suddenly felt like a giant ass if he started to act less than gentlemanly. I had used it plenty of times. The only problem with my move was that it only worked on men that were generally well behaved. If I misjudged a man and he wasn't respectable, then things sometimes got a little more difficult.

"Can I call you?" I said with a sweet smile.

"Oh, of course." He grabbed a pen and started to write down his number. "You call me anytime. I'd love to take you out on a real date."

"Thank you so much, George. I've got to run to work now. I'll text you," I moved in to kiss his cheek, but he turned and his lips touched mine.

I gave him a long, hard kiss in the hope that it paid off down the road, and maybe I could make something work with George. His place was plenty big enough to share, and it sounded like he worked a lot. It had been a long time since I had a regular boyfriend, but George seemed like a sweet guy and I definitely was considering him as a possibility.

As I left his apartment, I looked back and wrote down the apartment number, just in case I ever needed to drop by or something. It was December in New York, and there was no way I was ever sleeping in a shelter. George seemed like the kind of guy that would let Isabella and I crash on his couch if we were in desperate need of a place. The nice guys were the best ones to keep around.

"Isabella, answer your damn phone," I said to her voicemail as I walked toward the subway.

She had left with some jerk from the club, and I was worried sick about her. Isabella never made wise choices in the men she hung around with. Instead of looking at their financials and their ability to be sweet, she looked at their abs. I tried to explain to her that the hot guys were the ones she should stay away from, but she never listened.

Two minutes later, I got a text from her:

"Can't talk. I'm with the sexy rocker. See you later at Glance; remember we are doing the peep show together tonight."

"OK," I replied.

Glance GoGo Club was our fun place. We both worked real jobs during the day and at Glance in the evenings. It was fun, and we got to party and get paid for it. Glance wasn't a strip club, and both of us were highly against becoming strippers. Glance was a dancing club, and we got paid to dance on stage or in fun scenes. It wasn't Broadway, but it was something better than my boring waitressing job.

I finished buttoning up my plain white top and tucked it into my tight black skirt. I worked the morning shift at Henderson's on the Green. It was a restaurant in the lobby of the Ritz-Carlton and located on the south edge of Central Park. The breakfast crowd was my favorite, they tipped the most and there were often families. Rich families were much more generous than rich men alone. It seemed counter-intuitive, but I paid special attention to the wives and the children and always ignored the men. The wives appreciated that and tipped me well for it.

"You're late Abigail," my boss said as he wrote a note in his little notebook.

"Yes, I'm sorry Mr. Walden; I will stay late to make it up," I said with a smile.

"OK. Thank you. Let's try to be on time tomorrow."

"Yes, sir."

Mr. Walden was actually a really decent man. He had a wife and twin girls and worked his ass off at the restaurant. He was firm but fair, and I wanted to keep my job. Mr. Walden was the best boss I had ever had. He never tried anything with his waitresses and was extremely understanding with our outside lives. But his one sticking point was, he wanted us there on time. He couldn't make the guests happy if he were understaffed, so most girls were eventually fired because they didn't show up on time enough. I didn't want to be one of those girls.

"Table two is the Gioacchino family. Be especially attentive to them," Mr. Walden said.

"Who is he?"

"He's bad news. Not quite the mob level, but bad news. Just be prompt and smile," he said, returning to his office.

Mr. Gioacchino was handsome. He was older, maybe early fifties, but he dressed extremely hip. He had tattoos on his arms, with a short buttoned up shirt and loafers. His graying hair was styled long on top and shorter on the sides, and he had a perfectly manicured beard. I had never been one of those girls that chased after older men, but I would have chased after him for sure. Except he was married, and I didn't go after married men.

"Good morning, can I get you some coffee?" I said, looking right at Mrs. Gioacchino.

I smiled and kept eye contact with her. She was beautiful, at least, ten years younger than her husband. Mrs. Gioacchino was dressed much more conservatively in a suit and had her blonde hair pulled up in a bun.

"I'll take a black coffee," Mr. Gioacchino said.

I briefly turned to him and smiled, but then quickly turned back to his wife. Even that quick glance into his eyes had sent an enticing shock through my body. He was even more handsome up close.

"I'm not really sure what I want," his wife remarked.

"I'd suggest the cappuccino and a grapefruit, you look like you have business to do today, and they will give you energy without the drop later in the morning."

I smiled, and maintaining my posture, turned toward Mrs. Gioacchino. She was my primary client, and I needed to make her happy. No flirting with her husband. No side glances at him. Only continued eye contact and helpfulness to her.

"Oh, yes darling. Thank you, that sounds delicious."

"And anything else for you sir," I said as I looked at my notepad and tried to avoid eye contact.

"I'd like the house special, thank you."

"That girl is absolutely delicious, Aldo," I heard Mrs. Gioacchino say as I walked away.

I couldn't help smiling at her words. It wasn't very often that other women were kind to me. Even if it was in a weird, flirting sort of way. It was nice to hear kindness from another woman. Most of the women I was around were intimidated by me. They thought I was going to steal their man or that I was some sort of bitch that wouldn't be nice to them. I was always nice to the women I served at my tables, having learned that they were almost always the real ones in charge.

I wrote his order down on the move and then hurried to the back to give it to the cook. My co-workers stood there and stared at me as I returned to the back room. The look on their faces was ominous.

"You know who that is right?" Rob asked me.

"Yeah, Mr. Gioacchino."

"Wow, was he scary? Do you think he has a gun with him?"

"What are you talking about Rob?"

"He was charged with eight murders back in 2005. Eight, not seven, not six ... eight murders. He did them, but no one could prove it. Now he's apparently gone legit, but no way I'd ever want to be face to face with the man."

My blood went cold at the idea I had just served a murderer. He didn't look like a murderer, but then again, I didn't really know what one looked like. He certainly looked like a tough guy, and I would bet with him on any fight. Despite his age, he looked to be in excellent shape. But why would a murderer be eating at a fancy restaurant like ours?

"He seems like a normal family man to me," I said, trying to ignore Rob.

"Yeah, normal like ... hey, let me chop your head off ..."

I finished serving the Gioacchinos and made a special point to compliment the wife; I wasn't above flirting with a woman if it would get me a bigger tip. They gave me a hundred-dollar tip for their breakfast and seemed rather nice. Except for the whole past murdering thing, Mr. Gioacchino seemed like a good guy.

Chapter 2

THEO

"Get up!" I screamed at the man as he bled on the ground.

"She's a rotten whore," the man yelled up at me.

I grabbed him by his arm and yanked him into a standing position. Did he really think it was alright to talk about one of my girls that way? Did he really think I was going to be alright with it?

"You apologize to her right now," I said. "Kimberly, come over here so this man can apologize to you."

I watched Kimberly as she tried to stand up; her face was battered and bloodied. She looked about to fall over at almost any moment, but she was a good girl and struggled over to me.

"I swear to God, you better apologize to her or you're going to feel pain like you have never felt before."

I pressed my hand around his neck and held it tightly as I waited for him to come to his senses and decide he wanted to apologize to Kimberly. If my punches had not swayed him, though, I wasn't certain that the threat of strangling him would be much better. But sometimes the lack of oxygen was just the right fear for a man, and he would suddenly become remorseful for what he had done.

Violence wasn't something I enjoyed. In fact, I spent most of my life avoiding any sort of violence altogether. I was a businessman, though, and if word got out that I was alright with men roughing up my girls, then I wouldn't be known as the owner of a high-class VIP escort service any longer. Instead, people would think of me as a lowly pimp, and I couldn't have that.

I had worked far too hard and too long for the reputation that I had and wasn't about to piss it away on some jerk who didn't get what he wanted from a girl.

My girls were not required to sleep with the men that hired them. I made that perfectly clear to the men who paid for their services. They were not paying thousands of dollars for a high prices whore, they were paying for a high-class woman to be by their side for the evening.

Certainly, many of the men who hired my girls ended up getting lucky at the end of the night. But that wasn't any different than any other girl who went out on a date with a guy. If he were kind to her, polite and looked out for her best interest, the women would often reward their man. But if a guy was a jerk, or expected to get laid at the end of the night, well that just didn't work out very well for them.

Kimberly leaned up against the wall, but she refused to fall back on the ground. She was a tough girl; all my girls were tough. They had been beaten up before, they had seen some horrible things in their life. There was no way Kimberly was going to let a guy like Rocco Stevens get the best of her.

Many of the girls that came to work for me had worked as prostitutes before, some of them hadn't. But all the girls that I hired had a strength that I found appealing, and I knew the men that I worked with did too. Strong, confident women were sexy, and that's what guys paid thousands of dollars for. They didn't want the hassle of trying to find a woman for one evening with their boss, and they didn't want to worry about if she was going to cause a scene at a party they needed to go to for work; the guys that hired escorts were looking for simplicity. These men wanted smart, no-nonsense women that could hold a decent conversation and make them look good while out with their friends or co-workers.

Of course, all the women I hired were absolutely beautiful, each of them in their own way. Men had specific tastes, and I catered to all of those tastes. I had tall girls and short girls. I had blondes, redheads and brunettes; I even had a few girls that liked to color their hair in wild random colors. I had girls with big breasts and small ones, big asses, and tiny asses; I had a girl for any man and prided myself on the variety of women I had working for me.

I loved women. I admired them and worked with them to help them have the best life possible. When accidents like what happened to Kimberly occurred though, I always felt guilty. It was my job to keep them safe, and I had not done my job correctly if one of my girls ended up hurt.

Rocco just stared at me without the slightest bit of emotion; I knew I was going to have to strangle him. I really didn't like hurting people, but there was no other choice. He had left me with no other choice at all.

My hand tightened around his neck and I looked at him as he stayed unusually calm. Something was wrong; why wasn't he afraid of me? I squeezed harder. Normally, it was about this point when a man gave in and would apologize. Oh, it hadn't happened very often that I had to hurt someone, but when I did, I always got the apology my girl deserved. This guy was different, though, he didn't seem afraid of me at all. In fact, he seemed pretty cocky for a man who was being strangled.

His eyes bulged out of his head as he continued to stand still and not fight me at all. So I squeezed even harder. My hand pressed against his windpipe and I knew I was only moments away from taking his life.

"Stop Theo, you're going to kill him," Kimberly said as she grabbed onto my arm.

"Maybe he deserves to die for what he did to you?"

"He's Aldo's guy. Stop."

I looked at Kimberly and loosened my grip on Rocco. Aldo and I had worked together for many years; I didn't want to ruin that relationship. Aldo was the one who had gotten me into the business. He was a tough motherfucker though, and I knew he would have done the same thing to any guy who hurt one of his girls, and he knew better than to let any of his guys hurt my women.

"He wouldn't allow this behavior either," I said, still unwilling to totally release Rocco from my grip.

"It's alright Theo. He knows better now."

Rocco looked at Kimberly and then me. He nodded his head in affirmation that he did indeed know better now. I pushed him to the ground and gave him one swift kick to the gut.

"No more of my girls ever Rocco. You're done. And don't think because you work with Aldo that you're safe. He's just as much against hurting women as I am. When he hears about this, you'll be lucky if he lets you live."

I grabbed Kimberly and let her lean on me as we left the hotel room. She was hurt real bad, and I needed to switch my attention to her. It looked like she needed to get to a hospital right away, but I knew she wouldn't go.

It didn't often happen that one of my girls was hurt so bad that I was willing to take them to a hospital, but in this instance, I would have taken Kimberly. I was a businessman, and although I hated to admit it, Kimberly was a commodity that helped make me money. I certainly wasn't going to let her suffer and not take care of her. If she felt good, then she was helping me make money. The quicker she felt better, the better for business.

"Do you need a doctor?" I asked as we made our way out the back of the hotel to the hired SUV I had waiting.

"Yes," she said as her knees buckled and I grabbed her.

Kimberly was tough, and I knew she wouldn't agree to see a doctor if she wasn't genuinely hurting.

"Hospital or at my house?" I asked.

"Your house, I've got a warrant for stealing, remember," she said in a weak voice.

"I'll have the doctor meet us there; you're safe now. I'm going to take care of you," I said as her body went limp and she passed out.

I felt her weight in my arms, and the color drained out of her body. She was exhausted. She needed help and I was going to be the one to assist her. Never in a million years would I have guessed that I would end up as a father figure to dozens of women. But that's exactly what I was; many of these women didn't have a single person who cared what happened to them. It was my job to be that person.

It was a fine line that I walked between boss, friend and lover sometimes, but it was my life and I did the best I could. Many people would think that a guy like me didn't really like women at all. How could I help men buy time with them and still value a woman? But the truth was, I cared deeply about the women who worked for me. I only wanted success for them, and whenever any one of them decided to get out of the business, I was happy for them.

I had watched girls go off to college, get jobs on Broadway, and even become television newscasters. I was happy for every single one of them. I treated my girls with respect and expected all the men who spent time with them to do the same.

"Mario, call Jack. Tell him we need a doctor at the house right away."

"Yes, sir."

Mario was the best driver I'd had in many years. He was reliable and kept to himself. Mario always did exactly as I said and never questioned me. His ability to keep things confidential had moved him up from just driving the girls to their dates to now driving me. I even had him work as my private security guard when situations got a little out of control.

It was hard to find good help, and Mario was definitely that. I planned to keep him around as long as he wanted to work with me.

"It's alright Kim, just rest. I'll take care of you," I said as I laid her in my lap and we sped off to my penthouse.

I hated to bring the girls back to my place but couldn't let the other women see Kimberly and what had happened to her. If they understood the level of danger that was involved in the escort business, many of them would leave. The whole reason I had convinced them to work for me was that being an escort was safe. 'Being an escort isn't like being a prostitute,' I told them. 'Escorts are just girlfriends who don't cause emotional chaos.'

Although the escort business did have its occasional dangerous evenings, mostly it was a much safer business for women than even working at a local strip club. I screened my clients extremely well, or at least, I tried to. Recently, it had been more difficult.

I was getting older and looking at more legitimate business deals. Eventually, I hoped to get out of the business altogether, but the money was so damn good it was hard to leave just yet. I had the capital for my new adventures, but my new businesses were all still losing money. I needed to keep the escort business going until my other deals had started to make a profit.

Aldo had been my mentor over the years, and I had watched as he slowly got out of the illegal businesses and built up his legitimate companies. It was an essential part of growing old, I figured, and I would eventually have to make the transition.

My restaurant had started off to rave reviews and earned me a lot of press in the beginning, but that had mostly died down. The news stories had turned to my bachelor status and most articles were done as part of a 'Hottest Singles in New York' type of thing. I didn't turn down any interviews as any press was better than no press. But it was getting old trying to squeeze in tidbits about my restaurant and gym into articles. I had a manager who handled the day to day operations of the restaurant, but it wasn't turning a profit at all lately.

The gym I started was unique in that it was a place for trainers to bring their clients and work one on one with them. I didn't charge any fees to the clients to be members, and instead, charged only the trainers. They paid a flat fee to work out of my gym and bring their clients there. It had grown over the last two years, and there was a growing trend of other competition doing the same business model. But none of them were on the top floor of Merck Towers with 360-degree views of the city. My gym was by far the most glamorous and elite. I had a great trainer and office manager who took control of the gym, and it was growing each month. I had a lot of optimism about the gym, more so than the restaurant.

Soon, I would be able to give up the escort business, but for the time being, it was my sole income used to keep my other two businesses running. The public thought I was a billionaire from my investments over the years; some people thought I came from a rich family or I had sold a tech firm. But Aldo taught me never to answer questions directly about how I earned my money and instead point people to how easy it was to make money through investing. They thought my two businesses were funded with that money, but the truth was that I had made my money from my VIP Escort business.

We pulled into the parking garage of my building, and Jack was there waiting for us. He was my right-hand man and best friend. If it hadn't been for Jack, my business wouldn't be what it was. He turned my basic idea for an escort service into the top VIP elite escort service in the city. Jack took a lot of the day to day tasks off of my plate as I built up my legitimate businesses, so I was going to have to talk to him about the screening process for the clients. But we could do that later.

"How is she?" Jack asked.

"She's good. She woke up in the car, but she's really weak. Maybe a concussion or something? I'm not sure."

"The doctor is only five minutes out. Let's get her to the room."

"Sir, I can help," Mario said as Jack and I struggled to get Kimberly on her feet.

"Alright, help Jack get her upstairs," I said.

I held the door for them as Kimberly got to her feet and they held her up. She was pale, and her eyes were having a hard time focusing. It pissed me off that I hadn't done more to Rocco. I should have killed his ass for doing that to Kimberly. She was going to be out of work for a month at least, and although that money didn't mean much to me, it did to her. I made a mental note to talk with Aldo about recouping that money from Rocco for Kimberly.

"Thank you," Kimberly whispered as we laid her down in one of the spare bedrooms.

"How are you feeling?" I asked.

"My head hurts, and I feel like I'm going to throw up."

I grabbed the trash can, brought it next to the bed, then grabbed the wet rags that Jack handed me and started to clean up her face a little. I hated this part more than anything else I had to do with my job. It was disgusting when a man thought they could hurt a woman, and it made me sick to my stomach to see the wounds that came along with those horrible acts.

"Wait, just a second," I said, pulling my phone out. "I'm going to take a couple photos for proof just in case we need them. Is that alright?"

Kimberly nodded her head and lay back on the bed so I could take a few photos. I took one photo of her cut lip and cheek, and then one of the bruising on her arms and wrists. Then Kimberly pulled up her shirt, and I took a picture of what appeared to be a bite wound on her left breast.

It made me sick how a man would treat a woman like that. I didn't care if they were paying for her time or not. No man should harm a woman, no matter what. It was disgusting. These men came to me in search of the highest educated women, with manners and bodies that were insanely on point. How on earth could they not respect and admire the beauty that my women had both inside and out? I could never understand men that hurt women.

"He's here," I heard Jack holler as the doorbell rang.

The doctor made his way quickly to the room. He had been there before, only about a month prior. That time, the girl had been strangled by her date. He had convinced her to play an asphyxiation game and it had gone horribly wrong. In that instance, it was the man who called me himself. The girl had passed out and was really out of it when she woke up. He was a decent guy, and instead of leaving her there in the hotel room, he called me. It was a huge risk he took and I commended him for not being a total jerk and leaving her, but I still decided that he couldn't date any more of my girls. I just couldn't afford to have my girls playing those kinds of dangerous games.

The doctor closed the door and stayed in the room with Kimberly for what seemed like an hour. He sutured up her cuts and cleaned her wounds. He talked with her and got the full story of what had happened. Mostly because I didn't want to know that information, but also because I found that the girls preferred to talk to someone besides me when things went bad. They didn't want to lose their jobs and were fearful that I wouldn't let them keep working if I knew what had happened.

"How is she?" I asked as Dr. Benton came out from her room.

"She is not in good shape. You will need to keep a close eye on her. She has a concussion, broken rib and several wounds that required stitches. I taught her how to clean her wounds, but she is going to need to rest for a few weeks so that rib can heal."

"Of course, anything else?"

"No, but take her to a hospital if she starts vomiting or experiences any trouble breathing."

Dr. Benton didn't want to get too involved at all. He kept the details to a minimum and was quickly out the door and back on his way to his Fifth Avenue office building. The only reason he worked with me at all was because he had once dated one of my girls and it had gone extremely well for him. He had taken her with him to a class reunion and made every one of his college friends jealous. There wasn't anything like the look your friends gave you when you walked into a room with a smoking hot woman on your arm.

"I almost killed him," I said to Jack and Mario as we sat down on the couches. "What the hell happened Jack? That guy Rocco works for Aldo and did this to her. How didn't we know about this guy beforehand?"

I saw the shock on Jack's face and knew he felt bad for what had happened. I didn't want to chastise him, but he had to do better. He had to keep the girls safe. Since I had become so busy, I hired Jack to do a lot of the day to day work. He was supposed to deal with the girls and set up their dates, and it was his job to check the guys out before he agreed to allow a new guy to date any of our girls.

"I'm sorry, Theo; I didn't have time to vet him. It won't happen again."

"I love you Jack, but you need to make sure these girls are safe. We have had entirely too many assaults lately. How many girls down are we now?"

"Four."

"Mario, do you think you could keep an eye on Kimberly if Jack and I went out tonight?"

"Of course, boss."

"We need fresh girls, Jack. The holiday season is our best season."

I wasn't being crass, it was just part of the business. I was always looking for fresh girls and did my best to help out any girl when she crossed my path. But if I didn't get some fresh blood in the doors, my guys were going to start looking elsewhere, and I didn't want that.

Three of my girls had recently left to follow their dreams, and with Kimberly out of it for a little while, I needed to get a few other girls working and taking dates. It wasn't a hard job for the right kind of girl. But it was hard for me to find the right kind of girl.

Girls who were turning tricks weren't actually the best at being escorts. The girls I liked best were the smart ones. If a girl knew how to manipulate a man into liking her, it made his night great, and it almost always landed her a second date. Girls who really knew how to play the dating game and seduce a man were much more who I was looking for.

"There's one more thing," Jack said with a serious expression.

"What?"

"Aldo called while you were in with Kimberly. He wants to meet with you tomorrow. He didn't sound happy."

"Oh Jesus Christ, is he actually pissed that I beat up his man?"

Aldo and I went way back, but when he was angry, there was no telling what he would do. I certainly had worked hard to stay on his good side over the years, and I would have to go see him in the morning and explain what had happened. In my experience, Aldo wasn't the kind of guy who allowed women to get hurt, and I really believed he wouldn't fault me for what happened with Rocco.

Working with Aldo over the years had been a delicate balance. He was certainly the reason I had started my escort business. Without his knowledge and referrals, I wouldn't have made it to the high stature I was at. But I had to distance myself from him over the years because together we were just too big a target to our competitors.

It also didn't work well for either of us to be seen together when we were both trying to build up a legitimate business presence. We had to spend more and more time with our other business partners and less time around each other.

"Not sure, but I'd bring some protection with you when you meet with him."

"I'll be alright," I said, trying not to look concerned at all.

Chapter 3

ABBY

My feet ached horribly by the end of the afternoon. The day had been very successful for tips, and I immediately went to the bank to deposit it so my sisters could have access to the cash back in Wichita, Kansas.

"Sam, I'm putting two hundred dollars into the account so you guys can buy some groceries," I said when I called her.

"Abby, it's alright, we aren't going to starve to death. There are plenty of canned foods for us to eat still."

"Samantha, I won't have you two going hungry. Now tell me what you know about the bank? Have they contacted you guys?"

"I think Bailey talked to them earlier today, but she had to get to work, so I haven't had a chance to talk to her. She's working at The Chicken Shack now."

"Oh, that's good."

It wasn't good. It was horrible. The Chicken Shack was a rundown no-name fast food restaurant in town. It paid minimum wage and was hardly worth Bailey's time to go there. But I wasn't about to make either of my sisters feel bad for their jobs. They worked hard and were trying the best they could. Unfortunately, even with both of them working, they barely could pay the utilities, car insurance, and gas. I made more than them in one day.

The problem I had was living in New York was damn expensive. I had to keep up my appearance to keep my jobs, and the money I made went toward the day to day living needs I had. Isabella and I had a gym membership so we could shower easily, we shared a small storage unit for our clothing, and we always found places to sleep. An apartment would have cost us well over $2,000 a month and that just wasn't something we could afford.

I didn't normally make $200 in tips a day. I sometimes only made $30. Plus, I only worked three to four days a week at the restaurant and another three- or four-nights dancing. There just was never enough money. I kept thinking that if I worked harder, I would somehow have enough money to help my sisters save the family home, but it wasn't looking like that would happen.

"Have her call me when she gets home. Leave her a note in case you're asleep when she comes in. I need to know just how much money we have to pay to keep the house from going up for auction. I know we won't be able to save the business, but maybe the house."

"It's alright Abby. We can move into an apartment or something."

"Sam, you have a house that is paid for. You wouldn't have to pay a monthly payment at all, just the yearly taxes. We just need to get those back taxes paid so you can keep the house. I'm going to make it happen, talk with Bailey and find out how much time we have left."

"OK. You know we could always come out there and live with you."

My mouth went dry at the thought of my younger sisters trying to fend for themselves in New York. They both thought I had an apartment and was doing well. They had no idea I never knew where I would sleep from one night to the next, and I wasn't going to tell them.

I certainly wasn't going to bring them to New York and have them living the life I was living. It was better that they didn't see what I went through, and I just couldn't stand the thought of them being disappointed in me.

"Let's just get you guys situated out there for now. You know I love you, right?"

"Yes Abby, I know. I love you too."

"I'm heading into work now. I'll talk to you guys tomorrow."

"Goodnight Abby."

"Night."

I felt guilty as hell for leaving them back in Wichita, but New York wasn't the best place for them. I needed to get my own place with Isabella and then they could come out and visit first. But Bailey and Samantha were not big city girls.

They were small town girls, and I just didn't want to see them corrupted by the city as I had been.

I met Isabella outside of our gym so we could shower up and get ready to dance that night. We were doing a cool go-go number in some clear walled shower stalls up on the stage. It was going to be a lot of fun. Pretty much every night Isabella and I got to do our show together was fun.

Originally when I came to New York, I wanted to be on Broadway. I wanted to sing and dance and be a professional performer. But it was much harder than I could have known to get into one of those shows, and I just didn't have the experience I needed to do it. Instead, I was relegated to dancing at a go-go club in a swimsuit.

Being a go-go dancer wasn't like being a stripper. We got paid a flat wage by the club owner and didn't make tips like strippers did. But of course, there were many other perks to the job. We got to drink for free all night long, and we got to meet guys at the club. There were plenty of snacks around behind the stage so we never had to worry about dinner on the nights we worked, and we made a decent amount of money per dance.

"I think we should wear schoolgirl outfits tonight," Isabella said as we made our way into the locker room.

"Um, no."

"Why not? It will get the guys all hot and bothered."

"No. How about our gold bikinis?"

Isabella just rolled her eyes. She hated the gold bikinis because she thought she was fat. But Isabella wasn't even close to being fat. She had curves that all women had, and the guys liked that. Isabella was also a much better dancer than I was, although I would never admit that to her. There was something about her ability to make eye contact with the guys that always had them fawning all over her when the night was over.

I struggled to connect with most of the guys at the club. It was impossible to find a guy that I was even remotely interested in, so I often just went for the lame guy that I knew would be safe to go home with. My defensive wall was up so high that it was practically impossible for a guy to get me to talk to them or show any sort of emotions. But most of the time that didn't really matter because the guys were too busy looking at my body to care that I wasn't talking to them.

"I'm not a size two like you are. I don't look good in that bikini. How about the blue one? It looks awesome with our eyes."

"OK, I'll compromise. Let's go with the blue ones. But you really need to get over this body issue stuff. You are beautiful. Like smoking hot supermodel beautiful."

Isabella just rolled her eyes at me again. I could tell her a million times that she was perfect, and she didn't hear a single word I had to say. She was caught up in her own view of her body, and that made me horribly sad.

One of the reasons Isabella and I got along so well was because we could both put aside our typical personalities and perform when we were on the stage. There was an actress in both of us, and that bonded us together. No matter how we behaved off the stage, when we were together on the stage, we knew how to put on a hell of a show.

"Hey, I picked up an extra hour dancing on the side stage. Natasha called in. Will you stick around and wait for me? Don't run off with anyone; I want to hang out."

"I'm not making any promises," Isabella said with a wink.

We showered and got ready in under an hour, and then we were on our way to Glance Go-Go. It was in midtown, and neither of us ever wanted to splurge for a cab so we just walked there. It was good exercise since we never used our gym to actually workout.

Having a gym membership was a necessity if you didn't have a place to stay. We used the gym as our personal bathroom whenever we needed to get ready for a date or other event. It was close to our storage locker and open twenty-four hours so it worked out no matter what time of day we needed it.

Living in New York without an actual place to live was a tricky undertaking, but Isabella and I had it down. We knew how to get to and from places quickly, where to stash our clothes when we needed to keep them for a few hours and didn't want to walk all the way back to our storage locker. We even knew what to say at the local hotels if we wanted to hang out there for a little while without getting in trouble.

Where many homeless girls went wrong was that they tried to hide out when they went places. They would try and make it so people didn't notice them, which inevitably made people notice them even more. Isabella and I knew better, we walked into places like we belonged there, no matter what we were wearing. We made eye contact with the clerk or person at the counter, and we always had a story that worked well for the situation. For example, if we needed to wait at the Hilton for a few hours until work started and didn't want to wait out in the cold or walk all the way back to our storage locker, we simply said we were waiting for our father to get off work from the laundry area. No one ever knew who actually worked in the laundry area, and no one wanted to be rude and tell us we couldn't wait for our father.

The line was huge outside the club as we walked around to the back and went in. It was going to be a fun night; I loved it when we had lots of people. The energy was amazing, plus it gave me many more possibilities to go home with. Glance was a top club in the city at the time, and everyone wanted to be there. It didn't matter if it was the middle of the week, people always wanted to dance.

"Oh, my God. Pizza? Someone had pizza delivered," Isabella said as we walked toward the dressing rooms.

Sometimes there wasn't any food backstage and we had to pillage the bar for olives. But most of the time, we could find some protein bars, fast food, or pizza that people would share with us. Of course, we never told people that we didn't have a place to stay. But we always took advantage of free food when it was there.

"Wait until after our shower scene, you don't want to look bloated," I said, and then instantly regretted it.

I was always thinking of what would look best on stage, but I knew I shouldn't talk like that around Isabella. She already had body issues and would instantly berate me for not wanting to eat pizza.

"Oh Abby, just eat some damn pizza. Your flat stomach isn't going to look that bloated from one piece of pizza."

"I'll eat some when we are done. We will only be out there for an hour."

The way our night started off was we would wear our outfits and dance on the side stage for about half an hour. Then the main stage was cleared and our set was brought out. The DJ, Romeo, had a special club mix that we liked to dance to and would play it as we stepped into our showers. The mix lasted about twenty minutes, depending on how much scratching he was doing with it and if he added any other tunes in with it. It was a fast way to earn $100, and on some nights, we booked a couple different sessions.

"Hey, remember to turn around and let the guys see your chest. You're always shaking your ass, and they like to see the girls as well."

"I'm always afraid my tits are going to pop out of our outfits. I really need to buy bigger tops," I said as I held my breasts and shook them at Isabella.

"No, your tops are just the right size. Stop being so self-conscious about your body," Isabella said as she teased me with my own words.

"I guess we both have to work on our confidence." I laughed.

"OK girls, it's time to head out," Amelia said as she walked past with a clipboard.

Amelia was the assistant manager at Glance and the one we dealt with most of the time. She did the schedule and worked pretty much every night. The club was closed on Mondays, so we all had that day off. But I saw Amelia there pretty much every other day of the week. She was shorter than Isabella and had brown hair with glasses. It seemed like she wished she had a figure so she could dance, but instead took the job as the stage manager so she could be part of the whole dancing scene.

"Hey did you see any good looking guys out there?" Isabella asked.

"Oh yes. You know who is out there tonight? Theodore Stern, yummy!"

"The name sounds familiar, who is he?" I asked.

"He was rated one of the top bachelors in the city. Super tall, dark hair and handsome as hell. He owns that new restaurant PalStyle."

"Point him out to us later, OK?" Isabella said as she pulled me out onto the stage with her.

Although we got paid good money for dancing, our goal was to find a rich and good looking guy that we could go home with. My unicorn was a rich, good looking guy that could also hold a conversation with me. Most of the time when I found a rich guy, he was ugly. When I found a good looking guy, he was poor, and when I happened to find a good looking guy that was rich, he was an asshole. Was it that much to find all three in one guy? I supposed so since I had yet to meet such a man.

I liked to dance, but there was always that initial fear when I went out on stage. I would look around and see who was watching me, then I would just turn around and start to dance. I had lied to Isabella about being afraid my breasts would pop out. I really just didn't like people to see my face or for me to see theirs. It made me nervous, and then I couldn't dance very well.

The music pounded and the lights pulsed as we moved in our bright blue bikinis on stage. Only in New York City was it normal to have women in hi-heels and bikinis dancing along to the go-go music; well, maybe it would also be normal in Las Vegas as well.

The first part of our set was easy. We were relatively unknown to the audience, and there were no direct lights on us. We got to move and dance however we wanted. The club goers were also dancing to the music, and I often glanced back to see them watching us. They liked the go-go dancers, even the women in the club. Many of the girls watched us and then would copy our dance moves to impress the men they were with. It was just one of the many reasons the go-go club was so popular.

Romeo was great about giving us dancers a cue before our shows. He would come on the microphone and ask who was feeling hot that night. We had about two minutes to get over to the main stage and into our showers. That was when the adrenaline really started pumping.

The anticipation of what the water temperature was going to be was always the worst for me. Some nights it was warm and the shower would be steaming as we danced. Other nights, it was freezing cold and you could see our breath, and our nipples, as we danced. I much preferred the warm water to the cold.

I held my breath as I waited for the lights to come on and to feel the temperature of the shower. I said a quiet prayer that the water would be warm that night.

"Turn around!" Isabella yelled at me.

I reluctantly turned around to face the audience. It was so hard to be that exposed to the audience, but I quickly tried to get into character so we could put on an amazing show.

The people toward the front of the dance floor had seen the showers being brought to the main stage and were ready to watch the show. Many of them had stopped dancing and were just holding onto their partners while they waited. It was a pretty amazing set, and Isabella and I loved that we got to do the dance scene in the showers, they were by far the most requested by the club goers.

Toward the bar, I saw an amazingly handsome tall guy standing there with another man. They were both dressed impeccably with expensive button up shirts and slacks. I wondered if the tall guy was Theodore Stern or not. Either way, I made a mental note of the two men so Isabella and I could go find them later.

When the lights came up, I couldn't see anyone beyond the people right in front of the stage. The rest of the audience would flash into focus every now and again as the lights pulsed, but not enough to actually see anyone.

My body was comfortable with our dance, and I instinctively moved to the music. We had performed our shower dance dozens of times. Each move had been perfected. Our timing was almost perfect as we let the music guide our bodies.

The water was warm, and I loved it. I felt sexy in the warm water and more sensual than when it was cold. I let my hands rub up and down my curves as I thrust my body into each of our moves. The dance was sensual, but it was more erotic than when we danced on the side stage.

It was a show for the audience. We were there to entertain them, to entice them, to make them want to be us, or want to be with us. Our jobs as go-go dancers were to entertain, and we did our best to make sure that happened.

As our song came to an end, I heard Romeo ask the audience if they wanted to see more of us. I silently swore at him for dragging out our twenty-minute dance. We got paid the same amount no matter how long the dance was, and I still had to work an extra hour on the side stage when we were done. The longer our featured dance took, the less of a break I was going to get before I had to dance again.

"Do you want to see Abby and Isabella dance to another song?" he yelled out.

I had to fight the anger as it welled up inside of me. He wasn't supposed to do that. We were paid to dance for one hour. If he played another song, it would go for 15 to 20 more minutes. It was exhausting to dance for an hour straight, and an extra 20 minutes wouldn't be paid for by the club.

I looked over at Isabella, who just shrugged her shoulders. She didn't care. Isabella was happy to give away her time and energy, but I wasn't. I had signed up to dance for another hour on the side stage. It was already going to be tiring enough. I would have walked off the stage, except it would look bad on me and I didn't want that to happen. But I would surely talk to Amelia and Romeo when I was done working.

When Romeo finally ended our show, I was exhausted. Instead of having 30 minutes to rest before I had to dance again, I only had 10 minutes. I was soaking wet and not happy at all with him, or with Amelia for letting him do shit like that.

"I'm not sure, but I think I saw that Theodore Stern guy standing in the back next to the bar. He had a friend with him," I said to Isabella as we dried off backstage.

"You can have Theo," Isabella said. "I'll check out the friend. You know I don't like super tall guys. They make me feel like a midget."

We both laughed. Isabella wasn't that short, maybe around 5'4" but I was four inches taller than her. So, I always took the tall guy, and she took the other one when we found a pair of bachelors.

"I'm going to be exhausted. I don't know, maybe I won't bother."

"Oh, I'm going to find this Theo guy and I'll get him all warmed up for you. Then you can just walk your sexy ass out there and take him home."

Isabella made me laugh. She had this ability to act confident when it came to men, but I knew deep down she was really self-conscious. If a guy criticized her, it hit her very hard; if he complimented her, she felt like it was the absolute best thing in the world.

"See you in an hour or so," I said as I slipped into a new outfit and brushed my hair out.

Chapter 4

THEO

"That blonde in the shower, we need her," I said to Jack as we waited for the show to start.

I'd had my eyes on both the blonde and the brunette next to her since they came up on stage. I needed another blonde; they were by far the most requested escorts. Every foreign traveler wanted a blonde-haired American woman by his side while he was in town.

The blonde was also short enough that the foreign guys would like her the most. It was sometimes hard to match up a Japanese businessman who was only five feet five inches tall with a girl that he would feel comfortable around. I had to have short cute girls around for them. It was also great to have girls that weren't stick thin all the time. Although most women thought they had to be perfectly thin to attract guys or work as an escort, the truth was that a woman with curves always got more dates. Guys liked curvy women.

The brunette, well that one I wanted for myself, at least at first. She could move into the escort business later, but I wanted my time with her. My body instantly reacted when I saw her on stage in that shower. My cock pounded full of blood as I looked into her brilliant blue eyes. We were at least 50 feet from the stage, and I could see that her eyes were blue, that was crazy.

Normally I didn't sleep with the girls that I wanted to hire, but I couldn't stop myself from thinking of this girl naked. I even imagined the possibility that I wouldn't try to recruit her at all.

I didn't have much time for real dating, though, and it wasn't likely any woman would be understanding of my business. So most of the time, I just couldn't date like a normal person.

She moved with much more shyness than her friend, so I doubted I would be able to convince her to be an escort right away or maybe ever. But that was fine with me if she decided she didn't want to do that; I'd be happy to keep her for myself.

It struck me as odd that I kept thinking about having the brunette for myself. Normally, that just wasn't me. But there was something about that girl that sent my nerves into overdrive. As I watched her move on the stage, I couldn't stop thinking about what it would me like to have her riding my cock.

"You want the brunette too?" Jack asked.

"I'm not sure. She looks pretty timid."

"She's on stage, in a shower, dancing for a thousand people. What exactly about that makes her seem shy?"

"I'm not sure. There's just this disconnect with her. I bet the blonde will say yes right away. You go after her. I'll work on the brunette."

"Alright Theo, but try not to get swept up in those eyes."

"I know, they are crazy blue." I agreed that it was possible for me to get swept up in them.

I had to laugh. Jack knew me so well. I loved a woman's eyes. They were a powerful entry point to her soul, and I felt like I could tell a lot about a woman just by how she looked at people.

Confidence wasn't all about how you looked or talked, there was a lot to say for making eye contact with someone. When I talked to potential women, I always paid attention to their eyes and if they could maintain eye contact. Someone who couldn't even look me in the eyes, wasn't going to do as well as a girl who could maintain eye contact and have a conversation. As much as men liked curves on a woman, they liked a woman who could hold a conversation too. Most of these guys were hiring a girl to take with them to a special event; they wanted a woman who would wow their friends and make everyone jealous on every possible level.

When the dance was over, I sent Jack to the stage door to watch for the girls. He could get them and bring them back to me. I never liked to seem as though I was the one chasing after them. But Jack didn't really mind it at all. In fact, I think sometimes Jack liked that he got to pick the girls out and bring them to me. But on this night, I had already decided that the brunette was going to be mine.

About fifteen minutes passed, and I noticed the brunette was back up on stage. She had changed into a tiny little dress, and her hair was combed out, but it was definitely her. There was no hiding her brilliant blue eyes.

She looked tired as she danced on the stage off to my left. I watched her face for a moment before she turned around and faced the back of the stage. Her ass moved with the beat, and I felt my cock throb with a desire to slide inside of that perfect round ass of hers. She had my full attention, and I didn't look away for the duration of her dance.

The white dress glowed in the club lighting, and her curves were shown off perfectly. I was mesmerized by her body as her dance moves enthralled me. It was more than just a dance; I felt her body like it was up next to mine and imagined what it would feel like to have my hands on her as she danced. Oh, I was certainly going to get my hands on that body later that night.

"Hey Theo, this is Isabella. Her friend Abigail is the brunette," Jack said.

"It's nice to meet you, Isabella. You are absolutely stunning, but I suppose Jack has already told you that," I said as I shook her hand gently.

"Hi, it's nice to meet you, too."

"We are going to go dance, I'll catch you later," Jack said as he pulled Isabella away.

Jack seemed to be pretty into Isabella as they ran off to the stage, but then again, Jack fell for all the girls he helped recruit. He couldn't help himself and constantly thought each and every one of them was the next love of his life. The problem was when they started working as escorts and making money, they all moved on and left him. It was a sad cycle, especially since Jack always talked about wanting to get married and have babies. He was a married guy trapped in a single guy's lifestyle.

"Grab Abigail for me when she gets done. She has another forty-five minutes," Isabella said as she moved behind Jack toward the dance floor.

Another 45 minutes? That sounded exhausting to me. I was impressed, though. This Abigail had some serious stamina if she could dance for as long as she had been. I wrestled with the idea of just recruiting her instead of flirting with her. The men would love her for sure. Her tight body, big tits, and those fucking eyes. She would be one of my top earners in no time at all. The key would be her personality; if she had a good personality, she could work for the really high-end clients.

My top girls were smart, classy and sweet. They were the combination of every man's dreams and could have a conversation with almost any type of guy and make him feel special. I'd wait and see if she was able to keep a good conversation; if she could, then I'd have to put her into the rotation. If she were a ditzy girl, I could keep her for myself to play for a bit before I put her into the rotation.

I was tired just watching her, but when she finally got off the stage, I felt the anticipation as I watched the side entrance. It was a good half an hour before she came out, though, and I was about to explode with anticipation. I had totally lost track of Jack and Isabella, but that didn't matter. I would be just fine getting Abigail to talk to me without them. Women had never been an issue for me.

"That was a long night of dancing; can I buy you a drink?" I said as Abigail walked toward the bar.

"Yes," she said.

Her brilliant blue eyes looked at me, and she didn't look away. I was captivated by her. On stage, she had seemed shy and hesitant; yet in front of me, she had confidence that I was totally unprepared for.

Her eye contact was intense as she stood next to me and looked right at me without looking away. She smiled slightly and seemed amused by my efforts to flirt with her. I suspected she had guys flirting and buying her drinks every single night.

"What can I get you?"

"Vodka."

The surprise on my face was obvious, and I saw a smile flash across hers. Most of the women I talked to weren't into drinking such a hard liquor. They typically liked fruity mixes or wine spritzers. This girl was a woman after my own heart going straight for the hard stuff and not pulling any punches.

"That's a mighty strong drink," I said. "Any mixer in it?"

"Some ice."

"Ha, okay then."

"I'll have two vodka's on ice," I ordered from the bartender.

She had hardly said five words to me, yet I was totally in awe of her. Typically, women who knew who I was would start gabbing about seeing me in some magazine or some other story they had read about me. The women who didn't know who I was were equally as chatty but about random other things. Silence just didn't seem to be most women's strong suit. But Miss Abigail had a mastery of the silence game that I hadn't seen in a long time. It fascinated me, intrigued me, and made me want her even more.

When our drinks arrived, Abigail drank hers straight back without even flinching. I followed suit and downed mine right after her. I liked this girl. I liked everything about her. It was so strange; I didn't know a damn thing about this girl yet felt so comfortable with her that I couldn't even describe it.

"Hi, I'm Theo. Your friend Isabella said I should keep an eye out for you. Abigail, right?"

"Abby," she said with a smile.

"You are mesmerizing," I thought and said at the same time.

"Thank you, Theo."

She smiled at me as she leaned up against the bar. Her eyes continued to look into me. Not at me, like most people did, her eyes looked right through me. I didn't care what other conversation we had that night, there was no way I was giving her up. She was going to be mine.

"Are you tired? We can go sit if you'd like."

"Yes, that would be nice."

Holding out my arm for her to hold onto, I led her to the back corner table that I'd reserved when I saw her onstage for the second hour. I knew enough about women to know that two hours in hi-heels and dancing was going to leave her ready to put her feet up. Sure, I thought it would be impressive that I had a table waiting for her, but I genuinely wanted her to feel comfortable.

As I slid into the booth, I stayed on the edge so that Abby could decide where she wanted to sit. She could sit across from me on the other end of the booth or she could slide around and sit next to me. I was eager to see where she decided to sit.

Her eyes continued to gaze into mine as she sat across from me; a little disappointment filled my chest. But at least, I would be able to gaze into those amazing eyes as we talked. It would be much harder to talk with her though since the club was so loud.

For the first time in a very long time, I felt nervous as I sat there with Abby and tried to talk to her. It wasn't like I was the type of guy who normally got nervous around women, but Abby made my nerves stand at attention, as well as my body. She was beautiful and sexy as hell. She had confidence and looked me in the eye like we were equals, and I felt like we were. Normally when I was with a girl, I felt better than her. Not because I actually was better than anyone else, but because of the way they held themselves around me.

If a woman seemed timid or shy, it was normal, but if she was shy and wouldn't answer questions with confidence, it made me feel like she couldn't hold a conversation at all. But with Abby, I felt like I was the one who needed to work on impressing her. My normal games weren't going to work on a girl like her; I could tell that right away.

Then I felt it. She had taken off her shoes and placed her feet between my legs on the seat. My cock thrust into full erect status as one of her feet accidently brushed against it. Oh fuck, I wanted to grab this girl and throw her over my shoulder and carry her right back to my apartment. Every nerve in my body was on full alert, and I couldn't get enough of her. The confidence she had around me was seductive and mesmerizing.

"How long have you worked here?" I asked in a louder than normal voice so she could hear me.

I moved my hands down to one of her feet and started to massage it. The look of bliss that rushed across her face was undeniable. My hands worked roughly into her foot muscles as I waited for her to answer me. Never in my life had I given a woman a foot massage, and I don't know why I decided to give Abby one, but the feeling of giving her any sort of pleasure was well worth the small amount of effort on my part.

"Two years."

"Are you trying to be a dancer on Broadway?"

It was a reasonable question. Many of the women I worked with were trying to make a life as an actress, singer or dancer. Some had other career goals, but I figured since Abby was dancing at the go-go club, then she probably wanted to be a dancer.

"Actress or dancer, but yes; Broadway. What do you do?" she asked, moving her other foot up to switch places so my hands could rub it as well.

Her confidence never wavered, yet I still felt like deep down she was shy. She held herself with confidence while we sat there in the booth, but on stage, she hadn't looked so sure of herself. Abby was a delicious mix of everything I loved in a woman, and I couldn't wait to get to know her more. But there was a nagging issue that I had to deal with. I couldn't bear to tell her that I owned an escort business. A girl like her wasn't going to keep talking to me if I told her; I could tell it in her eyes. She probably got hit on by dozens of men each week, and I would instantly be put into a category of a loser on telling her, so I didn't.

"I own a gym and a restaurant."

Abby just nodded and then sat and looked at me. She had a small smile on her face, and I was so mesmerized by her. The more I looked at her, the more I wanted to know about her. How did she get to New York? Where was she from? How old was she? I needed to get her out of the club, but I suspected that was going to be more difficult than with typical women.

"Where did Isabella go?" Abby asked as she looked out to the dance floor.

"They were dancing."

"Well, she's a big girl. I guess I'll see her later. Thanks for the drink," Abby said as she started to get up from the table.

She stood next to the table and reached under to grab her shoes. It took me a moment to figure out what was going on, but it looked like she was leaving me. I had never in my life had a woman just get up and leave like that. But before I could stop her, she had her shoes back on and was walking out to the dance floor.

I sat in the booth for a second as the moment sank in. We were talking, I rubbed her feet, she asked what I did for a living, and then BAM, she got up and left me there. Most women would have fawned all over a guy who owned two businesses. But as I quickly learned, Abby was not like most women.

I ran after her and caught her right in the middle of the dance floor.

"Was I boring you?" I said, holding onto her arm gently.

"I wanted to dance, and you didn't seem like the type of guy who danced."

"So you were just going to leave me there like that? You might never have saw me again if I hadn't chased after you."

"I knew you would come after me," she said with a grin.

Man, this girl had me. She was cocky and funny and nothing like the women I normally met when I was out at the clubs. I honestly couldn't stand the idea of her walking out of my life. A pull in my gut told me I needed to do everything in my power to keep a hold of this girl.

I laughed as Abby started to move to the music. Her hands pressed against my chest and her fucking blue eyes hypnotized me. This girl was by far someone I hadn't expected to meet. She was confident and mysterious; she seemed well educated and classy. I should have convinced her to go into the escort rotation. Men would have paid top dollar for her, I was sure of it. But I wanted her. I couldn't give her up. I wanted her so bad, I could feel my pulse pounding throughout my body.

Her touch was gentle and could have been innocent, but I felt like it was extremely erotic. She started with her fingers on my cheek and smiled at me as she traced a line down the side of my body. She stopped and wrapped her fingers around my biceps before moving to the waist of my pants where she tucked her fingers in slightly and pulled me toward her.

I was caught off guard by this woman. She had me wrapped around her finger, and I couldn't look away. Every part of me wanted her. I wanted to kiss her, to touch her, to lay her naked body in my bed and make love to her for hours.

My breath was shallow as I watched her to see what she would do next. I felt so out of my element. Abby wasn't like the women I normally met. She appeared much more put together than the girls that normally worked for me.

Suddenly, I wished I was totally legit. I wished I didn't run an escort business anymore and was actually just a restaurant and gym owner. I had to keep my escort business a secret from this girl. There was no way I could tell her about it; no way she would want to be with a guy who was part of a business like that. I knew I would have to keep my secret if I wanted to keep Abby around at all.

Abby wasn't the kind of girl that would just go home with any guy. I could tell she had much higher standards than that.

Chapter 5

ABBY

It took all the acting skills I had to keep my shit together as I talked with Theo. I couldn't look like some desperate dancer who just wanted a place to sleep for the night. My approach was simple. I was going to be quiet, confident and aloof. Shock him with the opposite of what most girls in clubs acted like.

A good looking and rich guy that could actually hold a conversation had just fallen from the skies and landed right in my lap. I didn't want to mess things up. For the first time in a very long time, I had butterflies in my stomach as I talked and danced with Theo. He was the kind of guy I had fantasized about finding, but I didn't want to be that girl who latched onto a great guy and scared him away. There was a delicate balance to catching a guy, and I had to work every single skill that I had.

The main problem that I had was Theo was so fucking handsome I could hardly keep my shit together. I was wet with excitement as his hands had massaged my feet. Who does that? What guy actually pays for a booth and offers to massage a girl's feet at the club? I couldn't decide if he was thoughtful or just a player who got lots of girls. He was certainly smooth and very attentive.

I admit that I always looked for the negative in guys. There had to be something wrong with them. Especially if a guy was still single in his thirties, that's when I knew he had some sort of secret or weird quirk that must turn the women off. New York was filled with gorgeous women, who were also smart and had great jobs; if a guy made it into his thirties without landing one of these women, I was instantly on alert. But I just couldn't figure out what was wrong with Theo.

It didn't really matter to me if he was a player, I could play that type of guy better than they could play me. But if he wasn't a player, if he was a sweet, normal guy, I wanted to play the potential girlfriend card. I was desperate for some stability in my life, and a steady boyfriend with money was the perfect opportunity.

"You are so beautiful," Theo said, pulling me close to him on the dance floor.

I let him pull me and I watched the desire in his eyes as I felt my body press against his. He didn't look like the player type of guy; he looked like a guy who usually got what he wanted, though. The way he held himself so confidently, he certainly wasn't like the guys I normally went home with. I didn't know for sure how I was going to handle Theo; all I knew was that I definitely wanted him to handle me.

My body tingled next to his, and I wanted him to touch me everywhere. The lust that moved through my body was hard to slow down, but I had to slow myself and my urge to sleep with him. I knew the rules of engagement when it came to single life in New York City and sleeping with Theo on the first night would get me absolutely nothing in the end.

Rushing off to his bed would get me a place to sleep for the night but not anything else. I had to behave myself. I watched him and tried to figure out what he wanted, what he liked. He was an enigma, though. The go-go club seemed beneath a guy like him, and I felt like something was off with the whole situation. A restaurant owner and gym owner would meet plenty of women at his businesses; he didn't need to pick them up at a dance club. Unless he just wanted someone for fun.

That was it!

He wasn't looking for a girlfriend or a one-night stand; Theo was looking for someone fun to hang out with, and someone who wouldn't push a relationship on him. Perhaps he was looking more for a friends with benefits situation. That was something I could agree with; I liked the sound of that better than all other options.

Of course, I wasn't positive of my analysis of him, but it was my best guess. Right away, I decided to back off of my aloof stance and play the fun girl. My acting skills came in handy when I was with a guy; it gave me the opportunity to mold myself into just what they wanted. If Theo was looking for a fun friend with benefits, I was just the right girl for the situation.

I hated the drama of real relationships and the uncertainty of one-night stands. It would be the best possible scenario if I could find a nice guy that I could play the friends with benefits card. In a relationship like that, you were only worried about having fun and hanging out. Sure, you slept together, but it was fun and without commitment. I couldn't do commitment; I was sure of that. I had yet to meet a guy that I would ever think about committing to in a long-term thing.

"Thank you," I said as I wrapped my arms around his neck and surprised him.

A smiled flashed across his face, and he held onto me even tighter. I felt like I was right on track with the 'fun' idea, and so I moved forward with my plan. It was nice to see him smile, and it looked damn good on him. But so did the aloof rich guy attitude he was doing earlier. To be honest, pretty much anything that Theo did was going to look damn good.

The music bumped loudly, and we moved together with it. It was loud and hard to hear each other, so dancing was the best thing we could do. I loved to dance, obviously, I did it for my job at the club, but even when we weren't working, I liked to come in and dance. When I was dancing, I felt free and like there wasn't a care in the world. Dancing was a way of releasing all my tensions and just letting go.

My eyes met his, and his smile continued as he looked deep into me. You could tell a lot about a man from his eyes, and Theo seemed the kind of guy that I would like to end up with someday. Of course, I wasn't delusional enough to think a guy like him would run off with a go-go dancer. But maybe someday when I got a job on Broadway, I would be able to find a man like him again. I didn't like to think about the long-term or ever settling down because it just wasn't an option for me yet. But at that moment, I let the thought run through my mind.

The constant eye contact was making me nervous, so I turned around and pressed my ass up against him as we danced. His hands slid up and down my back before moving to my ass and holding onto it. I felt his cock get hard, and he pulled back away from me so I couldn't feel it anymore. Secretly, I didn't mind feeling Theo's hard body pressed up against me. Normally, though, it was a huge turn off when a guy made it so well known that he was hard for me.

If a guy pressed his hard cock up against me when we first met, that said a lot about the guy as well. A jerk would have kept his hard-on pressed up against me to let me know just how excited he was. But Theo seemed to be a bit of a gentleman, and I was impressed. Everything about Theo had impressed me so far, and I was still looking for that fatal flaw that would let me toss out all ideas of having him for more than a fling.

"Abby!" I heard Isabella yell from about ten feet away.

She was dragging a guy with her that I recognized as Theo's friend. Isabella looked really happy with her guy, and it made me smile instantly. She was always trying to find her prince among the guys we went home with. I really wanted her to find him but doubted it would be at one of the dance clubs we frequented.

"That's Jack," Theo whispered into my ear.

His breath on my neck sent desire rushing through my body. I involuntarily leaned back against him and let my hand move up to his cheek. My breath caught as I waited for him to move his lips anywhere near my ear again.

As I arched my back and pressed into him, I felt his body as he gently pressed up against me. His hands wrapped around my hips and tugged me closer for a brief moment. It felt like I was supposed to be there with Theo. Everything in my body felt perfect. I didn't have the underlying feeling of wanting to run away and didn't want to be anywhere but right there with him.

"What?" I said, purely to get him to whisper in my ear again.

"Your friend Isabella is with my friend Jack. They look cute together," Theo said slowly.

His words were deep and deliberate, and I wanted to hear more. I wanted to keep my body firmly against his and let him speak to me for hours through whispers in my ear.

"Abby, this is Jack. We are going to go for a walk. I'll call you tomorrow, OK?" Isabella said as she hugged me.

I had to pull away from Theo to hug Isabella. I also had to talk to her and didn't think I was going to be able to pull her away from Jack long enough to have a conversation.

"He's too cute for me," I whispered into her ear. "I can't sleep with him."

"You can, and you will. Stop with the rules. Just go have fun for once."

"Bella, you know how easily I fall in love. I can't do it."

"For Christ's sake Abby, then fall the fuck in love. You can't spend your whole life avoiding men because you're afraid of love. Now I'm going to go hang out with Jack. He's got a line on a sweet gig that pays insanely well. I'll let you know what I find out. Take care."

Isabella kissed me on the cheek and then pulled Jack away from Theo and took off out of the nightclub. I hadn't been in love for a very long time, but that was because I purposely kept guys away from my heart. I found men that I knew I couldn't love and went home with them, instead of the guys that could possibly break my heart.

Theo and I stood there and watched them leave as we awkwardly tried to decide if we were going to go back to dancing or if we were going to do something else. I liked dancing with Theo. Mainly because I liked his hands on my body and the way he looked at me.

"Drink?" Theo asked.

"Only if we can keep dancing afterward," I said with a smile.

"Of course. Anything you want."

"Oh, anything?" I mischievously said.

"Yes."

"Another foot massage?" I teased.

"I'll massage your entire body if you'll let me."

"Maybe we'll try that later."

"Is that a promise," Theo said as we made it back to the bar.

"Sure. You dance with me, and I'll let you give me a massage. But you have to keep up with me. No lagging behind and trying to sit in that booth."

"I can keep up. I think it's you who will have the problem keeping up."

"We'll see."

Theo had ordered us a couple of shots, and we both downed them quickly. I liked talking with him and liked being around him. I felt myself letting down my wall when I was with him, but it scared me to death.

"Another round," Theo said to the bartender.

I winced at the idea of a third shot. I liked to be in control of myself. The third shot was just on the verge of me having fun and being drunk. But I went for it. Usually, I didn't drink much because I was afraid of what I would agree to do with a guy if I had too much to drink. But with Theo, I felt like I wanted to do every dirty thought that crossed my mind.

After one more shot, Theo pulled me back to the dance floor and I was hyped up and ready to dance. I kicked my shoes off and handed them to Theo and then went to work dancing intensely to the house beat. Theo did pretty well keeping up with me, and we were both drenched in sweat within thirty minutes.

His body felt good next to mine, and I occasionally reached up and let my hands run down his chest. I felt his hard pecks and abs under his shirt, and deep down I just wanted to slide my hands underneath his clothes and feel his skin. I had spent so much time chasing after the nice guys that I knew I could go home with and not have to sleep with that I hadn't spent very much time with a guy like Theo. A man that I was crazy attracted to and wanted to have naked next to me as soon as possible.

My mind spun with plans of what I should do next and how I should play the night with Theo. Then out of the blue, Theo threw me off.

He leaned in, grabbed me and pressed his lips against mine. My first response was to push him away, but then, looking at him, I knew I instantly wanted to do that again. So I pulled him back toward me. That made him very happy, and his kiss intensified as he dropped my shoes and held my face in his hands.

Our wet lips moved from one side to the next as we devoured each other right there on the dance floor. He was a good kisser, that was for sure. It was the first kiss I'd had in a long time where I actually felt my body wanting more and more.

"Water," I said as I pulled away. "I need water."

Theo smiled and pulled me behind him as we walked back to the booth. He sat me down and then went straight to the bar to get us some water. The club wasn't packed, but it was getting really hot, and I didn't want to turn into a dehydrated mess. I had certainly learned that lesson over the years and knew better now. Taking a break and drinking water was essential to making it through the night.

This time, when he returned, he didn't sit across from me; instead, he pushed me over and slid into the booth right next to me. He placed his hand gently on my thigh, and his lips moved right back into kissing me.

I didn't mind. In fact, I fucking loved kissing him. He smelt like a combination of Armani and old spice. I could tell he took good care of his body and I decided right then and there that I was going to sleep with this man. I didn't care about my plan to play coy or try to land him. My desire for him was much too strong for any plan.

"I'm glad I met you," I said between kisses.

"Me too. I had a horrible day today until I met you."

"I have special powers to fix any day and make it awesome." I laughed.

"I think you might be right."

As we sat close to each other, I felt a bond with Theo that I normally didn't feel when I was around a man. He was sweet and confident. That was a unique combination for me; plus, he was extraordinarily handsome.

His tall, thin frame had just the right amount of muscle on it; he had dark brown hair that was long enough for me to run my fingers through. And a gorgeous smile that I knew probably made all the girls wet with excitement when he flashed it at them.

"Why was your day bad?" I ventured to ask.

He mulled over whether to tell me or not, and I waited for him. I was perfectly comfortable with silence; it was my weapon in conversations with men. When I was silent, it forced them to talk. Most people didn't utilize the power of silence very well. Silence makes people uncomfortable so they fill it up, but if you can learn to enjoy the silence, it makes for a much better bond with the person you are talking to.

"Life isn't about the lemons; it's about the lemonade you make. Come home with me and make some lemonade," Theo said as his hand stroked up and down my thigh.

I couldn't help myself and burst into laughter. It sounded like the cheesiest line I had ever heard. But Theo looked so damn adorable as he delivered it.

"Does that line normally work on girls?" I asked.

"What line? It wasn't a line," he said as his face flushed with red.

"Oh, so it does normally work!" I exclaimed as I laughed more.

Theo rolled his eyes as I had just caught him right in the middle of what appeared to be some routine pickup line he delivered to women to get them to come to his home.

"Are you going to squeeze the lemons on me while you massage me?" I laughed.

Theo started to laugh too. It was fun to see that he had some humility about his horrible pickup lines. I was having one of the best nights of my life with this guy and certainly was going to go home with him. I didn't care if there was lemonade there or not.

"If it will make you happy, I'll make the whole lemonade right there on your naked body."

"Hmm, that sounds sticky," I said, pushing him out of the booth so we could leave. "Oh, crap. My shoes!" I said as I noticed I was still barefoot.

Without another word, Theo ran off to the dance floor to try and rescue my heels from a kidnapping fate that was sure to happen. I couldn't help smiling as he looked back at me just before he entered the dance floor craziness.

My eyes stayed peeled on the place where he had entered the dance floor, and I waited for him to return with my rescued heels. It was silly, but I hadn't met a man who so quickly understood how important a pair of heels could be to a woman.

I didn't have to explain it to him and didn't have to ask him to go look. Theo just ran off on the quest for my heels all by himself.

Throughout my life, I hadn't owned very many valuable things. When I was a child, I remembered a few cherished toys that I had to leave behind when we were taken to the foster home. Since I had arrived in New York City, I didn't have a place to keep very many things. Isabella and I rented a small 4x4 foot storage closet that we had organized like a walk-in closet. It was where we kept our valuable shoes and other items that we couldn't bring with us places.

It was a hell of a lot cheaper than an apartment and allowed us to spend money on the necessary clothing items so we could find good guys to take us out.

We certainly couldn't pick up high-quality boyfriends if we dressed like trash. It was essential that we had a few pieces of premium clothing. Whenever possible, we purchased items from our friends or at resale shops. We were frugal, and it helped us have a little variety in the clothes we wore.

But the Steve Madden heels that I had left on the dance floor were by far my most expensive purchase. I had saved up for two weeks to get them and swore they were the best purchase I had made. Guys noticed the spiky heels and used them as a conversation starter. They were unique, just like me, and I loved that.

As I continued to stare at the dance floor, I started to get nervous that Theo wasn't coming back. He had been in the crowd for a very long time. I moved closer to the dance floor and tried to peek through the crowd to see if I could see him, but the smoke and the sheer number of people made it impossible.

"What size?" I heard a voice whisper in my ear.

Oh, how I was starting to get used to his delicious voice in my ear. It was smooth and rough all at the same time.

"They were size eight," I said swinging around.

"I'll get you a new pair," Theo said as disappointment swept across his face. "It was my fault; I set them down."

"No, no, it's alright. They were old anyways," I said, trying to cover up the absolute terror of losing my $600 shoes.

"I won't take no for an answer. I'll take you to get a new pair in the morning." Theo smiled.

His hand weaved with mine and we walked toward the front door. It was cold out, freezing in fact. December in New York City wasn't exactly the best time to be walking around barefoot. Although I wasn't sure I would be willing to walk around New York without my shoes during any time of the year. I hesitated at the edge of the doorway, but before I knew what had happened, Theo had swept me up into his arms and was carrying me toward the black SUV that was parked out front.

"Oh, my gosh," I giggled as the people in line at the club watched us.

Theo had a driver waiting who opened the door before we got there, and with amazing ease, Theo slid me into his SUV. It was like a scene out of a fairy tale, and I was eating it up. For a moment, I thought that he might just be playing a game with me. Maybe it was all just one of the ways he picked up women, but then I realized I didn't care. I was going home with an extremely wealthy and handsome man who had been a total gentleman all night long. This was the kind of guy I had been waiting for. Theo was the perfect guy for me, and I was going to make sure he knew just how grateful I was for him coming along that night.

It was about time I had a little fun and got laid. It had been months since I had been with a man. But I had never been with a man like Theo. Someone so put together, handsome and funny. Theo was my dream guy, and I certainly wasn't planning on pretending to get ill when we got into bed together.

Oh, no, I was planning on letting his hands explore anywhere they wanted. I couldn't wait to feel his warm skin pressed up against mine as we made love. It was going to be one hell of a night, that was for sure. I was going to give Theo a sexual night he wouldn't soon forget.

Chapter 6

THEO

"Mario, you know my friend who was staying in the spare bedroom. How was she doing?" I asked.

There was no way around the fact that Kimberly was sleeping in my condo. I needed to set the groundwork right away to make sure that Abby didn't feel like something more sinister was going on.

"Sir, she was doing well. The nurse you hired had arrived and was taking care of her."

"Thank you, Mario," I said as I grabbed Abby's hand. "One of the girls who work for me was assaulted horribly by her boyfriend. She was afraid he had a key to her place, and I couldn't stand the idea of her staying in a shelter. She is staying in one of my spare bedrooms."

Abby looked confused, yet I saw her try to understand the situation and show empathy. Certainly, I wasn't going to tell her the woman was actually one of the escorts who worked for me and would have to talk with Kimberly to make sure she wouldn't tell either.

"That's horrible. Did they catch the guy?"

"Yes, they did. I'm sure he will get exactly what is coming to him, but sometimes they don't hold these guys for long in jail. She's going to crash with me for a bit."

"It is really sweet of you to take care of her like that. You are a better boss than any of them I've ever had," Abby said with a little laugh.

I really didn't know that much about Abby, but I assumed working at Glance wasn't very financially feasible for living in New York City. My estimate was that she shared a tiny apartment with a half dozen girls and everyone worked different shifts so they could sleep at different times in the house. It was a common story for girls who came to New York, and one that was perfect for me when I wanted to bring a girl into the escort world. Although, I very much wanted to keep Abby for myself.

Of course, Abby would make an excellent escort if she ever wanted to go into the business, and I was damn good at convincing girls to try it out. First, I would gain their trust. Then, I would show them what having money was like in New York City. It was what the girls had dreamed of, and often it was too hard for them to resist when I offered them a date with one of my friends.

That's how I started a girl in the business. I had different friends and clients that I trusted, who would take the girls out on their first date. They would wine and dine the women. Show them a great time. Typically, the women were so smitten with the men that they willingly hopped into bed with the guy. The next day, I would take the young girl out to breakfast, hand her a few thousand dollars and explain what her date had been.

At first, they were horribly angry. How could I trick them like that? they would say to me. But then as we talked, the girls would realize that being an escort wasn't any different than going on dates. Except for two things: the girls had to keep the drama out of the date, and they got paid a great deal of money for their time.

Abby would make a killing as an escort. Her slim frame, sweet smile and funny disposition were exactly what men looked for. Not to mention her knockout bright blue eyes; those would make her a fortune if she decided to give it a go. But I wasn't sure I was going to be willing to give her up. The idea of having a regular girl that was just for me was appealing, especially one that drove me wild like she did.

"I believe all men should protect and take care of the women around them. As a boss, boyfriend or friend to women; I'm always going to make sure they are safe and cared for."

"Awww, that's about the sweetest thing I've ever heard a man say," Abby said as she moved closer to me.

I watched as she rubbed her toes together and realized that they must have been absolutely freezing. Even though I had carried her to the vehicle, it was still

December, and it was still cold out. I reached down and pulled her toes into my hands and started to rub them again.

"Oooh, God that feels so good," Abby said with a moan after her words.

I saw Mario smile and look into the mirror at Abby and me, so I motioned for him not to look. He smiled and then moved his eyes back to the road in front of us. He was a good man and kept to himself. I didn't have to worry about him ignoring an order I gave.

"You must be freezing."

"No, I think all those drinks warmed me up just fine."

"Let me warm you up more."

I spread her legs around me and pulled Abby onto my lap. As she straddled me, I saw that damn amazing smile of hers and couldn't help but smile back. My hands reached for her and pulled her toward me as our lips locked together. I loved the taste of her, the sweet mix of vodka and what might have been strawberries or something else delicious. I just couldn't get enough and wanted more and more.

She tasted so good. She opened her mouth and let my tongue plunge into her as we enjoyed the soft touch of each other's lips. Kissing was something I didn't take lightly, it got me all worked up and I wanted Abby in my bed that very moment. It was hard for me to try and control myself and be a gentleman around her. Inside, I felt like a Neanderthal waiting to attack.

I wanted to let my fingers move up her skirt and feel her wet center but decided it wouldn't be the best way to gain her trust. And I needed her to trust me; I wanted her to trust me. Whether she was going to work for me or not, I had to have her trust if anything was going to move forward.

Being an escort might be in Abby's future, and I didn't want to throw away that possibility by pushing her to move too fast. I couldn't decide between keeping her or hiring her, and until I made that decision, I was going to have to avoid sleeping with her. Things got way too complicated when I slept with a girl before she became an escort for me. No. I had to behave myself at least for one night while I decided what to do next with Abby.

I saw the awe on her face as we made our way up the elevator to my condo. In New York, the higher your apartment was in the building, the more expensive it was. My condo was the penthouse on the 40th floor of my building. It impressed women, that was for sure. It probably hadn't been the wisest purchase of my life at $13 million. But at the time, I wanted it to show my status in New York. I wanted to throw parties and have people over who could be utterly impressed by my home.

The problem was, the New York elite didn't care about how expensive your condo was if you couldn't do something for them. Over the last few years as I started legitimate businesses, I learned that rich people always wanted something for nothing. They always wanted to come to free parties, get free meals and have free gym memberships. For me to keep giving away free things, I had to keep my escort business going. The escort business totally financed my legitimate lifestyle.

But I had stopped having parties at my home every week, and instead, just had one a couple times a year. I found that I actually enjoyed the peace and quiet of my home much more than I thought I would. Every now and then, I'd bring a girl home. A girl like Abby that I wanted to groom for the business and on the rare occasion I would bring a girl home that I wanted to date. Those girls took more time to warm up to the idea, so I needed to show them what life was like in New York when you had money.

"Well, this is it," I said as I opened my front door.

The city lights shone into the main room and brightened it up, even though no other lights were on in the room. I lived near Times Square, which was a bad choice of location for impressing the New York elite, but I loved it.

I loved the excitement of Times Square. I loved that there were people coming and going at all hours of the night. The excitement was energizing to me and gave me the drive to keep pushing forward on my next big project.

Abby made her way straight over to the floor to ceiling windows and looked out over the city. It was an impressive view, but I still loved to see the awe on people's faces when they got to experience it for the first time.

"Do you like it?" I asked, standing close behind her.

"No," Abby said as she turned around to face me.

Her comment caught me off guard, and I stood there stunned for a moment as I stared at her. She was a witty and funny girl that seriously made me laugh. I liked being around Abby and wanted to spend more time with her.

"No?" I laughed. "Why not?"

"It's too bright."

"Come with me."

I held her hand and walked her down the hallway. We passed Kimberly's room, and I made a mental note to check on her as soon as I had a free moment. When we got to my bedroom door, Abby hesitated for a moment, but I pulled her into the room with me. I didn't want to make love to her, I just wanted to show her something. Well, actually, I did want to make love to her, but I was going to deny myself that pleasure for the time being.

Instead of looking at the view, we walked right into the bathroom, and I started the water in the giant bathtub.

"Are you taking a bath?" Abby asked.

"Nope. You are."

"Um, I'm not taking a bath in a strange man's home."

I grabbed her and pressed her up against the glass enclosure to the shower. My hands pinned hers above her head, and I kept my lips about two inches away from hers. Intensely, I watched her to see what her reaction would be. Would she flinch and worry that I was going to hurt her? Would she press back? But no, she did neither; instead, she relaxed and let me look at her and enjoy the roundness of her lips.

Slowly, Abby licked her lips in what I had to assume was a deliberate ploy to entice me. I loved it. She was erotic, even if she wasn't trying to be. I felt my body lust for her, and my mind vacillated with possibilities. She would make a great escort. Her ability to go with the flow, to entice me already; that was something I couldn't teach a woman. But the problem I was having was that I wanted her so desperately. I wanted to feel her naked skin pressed up against mine and hear her moans as I thrust inside of her.

The problem was, I wasn't willing to give her up to other men. At least, not yet. I wanted her for my own. It really didn't happen very often that I met a woman I thought I wanted to keep for myself. But Abby was funny and witty, and that knocked me off of my game. A good businessman would have still recruited her, but I couldn't help imagining the possibility of her being mine.

"I saw you dance for hours on stage, then another couple hours with me. You've been walking in the freezing weather without shoes, and you look exhausted. I'm insisting that you relax and enjoy a warm bath. We can continue after you've had a chance to sooth those sore muscles."

Abby laughed at the thought of me giving up fucking her for the time being. I'm sure she had never experienced such a thing; a man who wanted her but wanted to make her feel good first. I was manipulative in my ability to get women to trust me; it was a special trait I had developed over the years. But the one key I had learned was to build trust. I could build that trust ten times faster if I refused to sleep with a woman on the first night I brought her home.

Another thing I had learned over the years was that women weren't appreciated nearly as much as they should be. Sure, I wanted to show the girls who worked for me what a man should treat them like. But most of the time, I didn't have a connection with a girl like I did with Abby. I purely wanted her to be comfortable and was genuinely willing to give up the idea of sleeping with her for the night if she wanted to just take a bath and go to bed.

Women expected men to be jerks. They have a long built-in history of men trying to get what they want from a woman as fast as possible. But whether I was grooming a girl to work for me or to live with me, I knew that not sleeping with her on the first night was an instant way to build up that rapport. I had to assume it worked the same way with a woman that I wanted to keep around for more than just a fling.

"Take a bath with me," Abby said as she started to undress me.

I pulled away. That was taking it too far. I couldn't refuse her if I were naked in a tub with her. I was a strong man, but even strong men had their weaknesses. If I felt her naked body pressed up against mine, there was no telling what I would do to her. I couldn't help imagining how delightful her skin would feel next to mine, though.

"You take a bath and relax. You won't be able to relax with me in there."

Abby moved her hands to my belt as her lips pressed up against mine. I was frozen there with her. The touch of her body made it impossible for me to leave her. Every inch of me wanted to feel her against my skin. Every nerve needed to have the excitement of her hands on it.

"I … think … you … need … a … bath … too," Abby said between soft kisses on my chest as she unbuttoned my shirt.

Fucking hell, there was no way I could walk away from her. Those deep blue eyes looked up at me as she slid my pants down to my knees. Her position had her lips directly in front of my throbbing cock as she removed the last bit of my clothing, and I stood still in anticipation of what she would do next.

If her lips wrapped around me, there would be no bath, no stopping me at all. I pressed my hips forward just a touch in the hope that she would take her pouty pink lips and wrap them around me. I wanted her mouth around my cock so desperately that my body ached for her.

But instead, she returned to standing and lifted her dress up over her head. Like a teenager, I fumbled to help her. But my coordination was gone as my body throbbed with a desire like no other I had experienced.

She teased me with her slow removal of each piece of clothing and her intense eye contact throughout the process. My body throbbed in reaction to her and pointed directly toward her. Oh, how I wanted to slide inside of her tight wetness. Oh, how I hated the idea of not sleeping with her, even for one night. One night without her seemed like an eternity, and I rushed to think through my plan again. Maybe it was a bad one, maybe living in the moment and showing her how passionate I was would be a better plan.

I laughed to myself at the thought. I had turned into one of my clients. Starting out the evening with no intention of becoming attached, then by the end of the night, I was willing to do anything to be with her. Whether Abby became an escort or not, she certainly was good at seduction. She had a skill that made me want to do absolutely anything to make her happy. I wasn't sure if this was a deliberate skill or not, but it certainly would be useful if she went into the escort business.

She turned around and bent over the tub to feel the water. My cock pointed directly at her ass, and it took every bit of my willpower not to grab her hips and thrust myself inside of her. I literally took a step back to keep myself from giving in. I had to decide what I wanted to do with this girl. Her seductive powers were intense and I could make so much money if she would come work for me; yet, at that moment, all I could think about was how much I would like to keep her.

"You need to get in that bath right now," I teased as my cock pulsed with an urge that I didn't know if I could control much longer.

"Oh, you don't like being exposed to my heinous naked body?" Abby said with a smile.

Her eyes were intense as she turned and walked toward me. I felt her hip press against my throbbing member and took a deep breath in as the touch of her skin shot through my body. I kept my hands at my side, trying to resist her. But soon I was going to give in; I couldn't last much longer.

"Yes, it's so horrible. Please hide it from me in the bubbles of the water," I said with a wink.

"You get in first," Abby demanded.

For reasons that I can't exactly figure out, I did as she asked and climbed into the bath. Her eyes, her naked body, my need to feel her next to me; it all collided, and I caved into my desires. There weren't many times in my life where I felt like someone else was in control, but there in that bathroom, Abby had total control.

"Yes ma'am," I teased her.

She climbing in and spread my legs so she could sit in front of me. I felt her hand reach back and grab my cock and push it up as her body pressed back against me. I thought I felt her stroke me just a little during the positioning of her body. But it could have just been my imagination since I wanted her hand to stroke me so desperately by that point.

I had never been so indecisive in all of my life when it came to a woman. Usually, I knew right away if I needed to sleep with her and pretend to be a boyfriend for a little bit before I got her into the business. But with Abby, I couldn't stop thinking about the possibility of keeping her and bringing her into the new legitimate world I had been trying to make for myself.

Could it even be possible to keep my escort business from her? If I wanted to take her to business dinners and fancy charity events; she would be the perfect date. But how could I date her and keep the sordid business away from her? It would be near impossible to do, especially with Kimberly living in the house with me at the time.

As Abby leaned her head against my chest and melted into a relaxed state in the tub with me, I knew I needed to keep her for myself. There was just no way I could give up such an intense connection. She had to be mine. At least, for the time being, I would keep her just to myself.

Now the hard part came … I needed to refuse her for the evening. I had to resist every nerve in my body and the urge to be with her. It would establish such trust in me, such unwavering trust; and I needed that if I was going to try and keep the secret of my escort business from her.

Keeping secrets wasn't something that I wanted to do. But the more I was with Abby, the more I was positive that she wouldn't want to be with a guy who ran an escort business. I had been planning to get out of the business anyways, there was no reason I shouldn't expedite that process and make it happen. Well, there was one big reason: money. The escort business was extremely lucrative and certainly the main reason I had a nice condo and the ability to start other companies. I wasn't sure I was ready to give up all that money yet.

Finally, I decided I would just have to lie to her and hope when the day came that she found out the truth; Abby would forgive me. She seemed like the kind of girl that could forgive a man if she loved him.

I couldn't believe the thoughts that were running through my head while I had Abby in my arms. Love, happily ever after, those weren't things I normally thought of, but my mind felt like a pile of oatmeal as I tried to think straight with her naked body pressed up against me.

Chapter 7

ABBY

"Okay, so tell me all about Jack?" I said as I sat with Isabella in one of the bedrooms of Jack's apartment.

"Oh, my God, Abby, I can't even tell you how perfect things are. He's so smart and not like the rest of the guys. I really think I could keep him around for a long time."

"Why? What's so great about him?" I asked.

I had heard it all before from Isabella. She fell for guys way too quickly, and I assumed Jack was just like the rest of them. She didn't see their faults at all and instead focused only on their positive traits. Isabella would ignore glaringly obvious issues only to look at something she felt was so good she could overlook the bad.

I tried to be a good friend to her as she went through boyfriend after boyfriend, but it was exhausting to watch her say the same thing about each guy and then have the same results. I really wanted her to find happiness, but I didn't think that was going to happen with a guy she met at the club.

But then I realized that I had also met Theo at the club, and I had fantasized that he might be the one for me. It was hard being such a romantic, but I did think that I finally had a small taste of what Isabella felt like when she fell so head over heels for the guys she met.

"He's rich, so let's start with that. Look at this place. Plus, he's helping me work, and I'm going to start making my own money. I said I wanted to get my own apartment, and he was all for it."

"Work? How is he going to help you work?"

"He's got a few friends that need a date for special events and stuff like that. I'm going to be their arm candy and get paid some serious cash. So if we want to get an apartment, you and I could do that now."

What Isabella was talking about sounded a lot like what I had just done with Aldo, and I suddenly didn't feel all that great about things. When Isabella said it out loud, it sounded a lot like being an escort, and that was the one thing I always told Isabella I wouldn't do.

We had friends that worked as strippers, and we even had friends that prostituted themselves out. None of it was what we wanted to do, and that was how Isabella and I had become such good friends. We both wanted more for ourselves and weren't going to sell

our bodies to the highest bidder. "So you'll go out with

these guys, and they will pay you?"

"No, they will pay Jack, and he'll pay me. Of course, he'll keep a fee since he is setting up the dates."

"So you're going to be a prostitute?" I said before I could stop the words from coming out of my mouth.

"No! Geeze Abby, not everything has to be horrible, you know. These are just nerdy guys who need a cute girl to go with them to something. Don't make it into a horrible thing. You know you could do this too and make plenty of money to send back to your sisters."

"I'm not going to be a prostitute just so I can send money to my sisters!"

"Let's calm down a little. No one is talking about sex here. For example, tomorrow I'm going with a computer salesman to his work convention. Nothing too exciting, I'm just going to help him talk to people and make his friends jealous."

"Sounds like prostitution to me," I said without thinking

about Isabella's feelings at all. "You're such a bitch

sometimes," she said as she stormed out of the room.

The truth of the matter was, I was feeling like a prostitute myself. Everything Isabella was describing was exactly what I had just done the night before with Aldo. I was judging Isabella for something I had done pretty freely myself. It was wrong, but I couldn't shake the feeling that I had crossed some sort of boundary that I had set for myself, and it was all because of money. Reluctantly, I made my way out to the living room to apologize.

"I'm sorry, Isabella. I need to tell you something," I said as I sat with her on the couch.

She had her legs pulled up to her chest, and I could tell I had made her feel like shit. It wasn't the first time we had fought, and it certainly wouldn't be the last time, but I did need to tell her the truth.

"What? Are you going to call me some more names?" Isabella said without looking at me.

"Theo took me to Vegas and bought me a bunch of shoes and dresses after we met. I didn't tell you because I didn't want to seem like a horrible person for taking them from him. Then when you told me about your day with Jack, I didn't know exactly what was going on, and I didn't want to make your day seem less special."

"Okay, so what? Theo is a nice guy with money just like Jack. I don't see anything to worry about."

"There's more. Theo introduced me to one of his friends who had a business event he needed a date for. I agreed to go with him last night, and he gave me this," I said, handing her the envelope with the $10,000 in it.

"Jesus Christ Abby! How much is in here?"

"Ten thousand dollars. You see, I was just saying those things because I feel horrible about my night, and I'm sorry. It was all about me and not about you."

"Did you sleep with him?"

"Theo? Yeah, I slept with him."

"No, the guy you went to the event with? Did you sleep with him?"

"No, his name is Aldo. But no, I didn't sleep with him."

"Then why are you getting down on yourself. You went on a date and got ten thousand dollars. That's much better than going on a date purely for a place to sleep for a night."

Logically, I knew that Isabella was right. I knew that what we had been doing before was pretty damn close to being an escort. But in my mind, there had always been a separation. In my mind, things were different, and I was an upstanding citizen who wouldn't sell herself for money. Unfortunately, I was starting to feel like I didn't have as great morals as I thought I had.

"I know. I just don't like this feeling," I said, holding my stomach.

I had crossed my own imaginary line, and it just wasn't sitting well with me. I didn't feel proud of the decisions I had made and certainly wasn't going to do it again. I had my own standards of what I thought was acceptable and wasn't going to give into them again, not for any amount of money.

"Stop it Abby. You stop feeling guilty right now. Your whole life has been you doing things for other people and not worrying about yourself. It's time you did what you had to for yourself and your sisters. This isn't any different than when we meet guys at the club and go back with them. In fact, this is much better. These guys want our company and are willing to pay for it."

"You know they want to have sex too, don't you?" I asked her.

"Well, so do the guys that we go home with from the club. You and I have skills, Abby. We can use those same skills to go on dates with these guys and get some serious cash. We don't need to sleep with any of them. Just use all the same techniques we have always used to get out of not sleeping with a guy if we didn't want to."

"Sickness, periods, emotional breakdowns ...I've used a lot of excuses," I laughed.

"Yes! You're much better at it than I am. Just use those

same things, and you'll be fine." "Maybe you're right."

"Maybe? Um, I'm always right; when are you going to learn this Abby,"

Isabella said as she hugged me.

We fought like sisters sometimes, but we always made up really quickly. Isabella and I were different, yet we both really fit well together. She was all I really had in New York City, and I wasn't about to push her out of my life.

"You know, I'm getting pretty pissed off at Theo though. He didn't say a damn thing to me at all about running an escort business or whatever it is that he and Jack are doing. He made me believe I was just doing Aldo a favor. What a jerk!"

"He didn't tell you he got the date for you?"

"Well, he didn't really get the date for me. I was with him when we went to his friend's business to talk to him. His friend, Aldo, invited me on the date to his business event and offered to pay me the ten thousand dollars."

"So this Aldo guy paid you directly?" "Yep."

"Then maybe Theo didn't set it up. Maybe this Aldo guy just really liked you. Perhaps he fell in love with you when he first laid eyes on you."

Isabella liked to mock me because one time a guy I had gone home with said he fell in love with me when he first laid eyes on me. He continued to text me and call me for weeks, saying that he was in love with me and couldn't stop thinking about me.

"Actually, I had seen him before. At the restaurant. He was that incredibly handsome guy who I couldn't stop looking at."

"Then he probably just asked you out on his own. Maybe Theo didn't want you to know about his business? What did he say he did for work?"

"I don't know; I think he said he owned a restaurant and made investments. So basically, he totally lied to me."

"No, I heard Jack talking about some problems with Theo's restaurant today. He definitely owns a restaurant," Isabella said.

I wanted to believe that what happened with Aldo and me had been spontaneous, but it was highly unlikely. I had not told Isabella about the

beautiful women and the envelopes of money that I had also seen over the last few days. But if Theo thought he could trick me into being his working girl, then he had something coming, and that was for a fact. I hated being lied to and despised anyone who would
purposely try to trick a woman into doing something she didn't want to do. At least, Aldo had been honest with me and talked to me like I was a partner in the night's events. Theo couldn't even be honest with me at all.

"Where is Jack at?"

"He had to run out. He'll be back soon and said that Theo

would be here shortly as well." "Oh, yeah, I don't think I

want to stay. I don't want to talk to him at all."

"You are going to stay here with me tonight, and I'm not going to take no for an answer. If you don't want to hang out with Theo, that's perfectly fine. But I won't have you at the shelter or anywhere else tonight. There's plenty of room here."

Jack's apartment wasn't nearly as fancy as Theo's, but it did have three bedrooms and seemed plenty big enough for Isabella and me to stay there. It made me a little sick to know that Jack and Theo were making so much money off of selling women to men who wanted to buy time with them. I couldn't get over the feeling that they were just glorified pimps.

"Are you and Jack dating then?" I asked as I looked down the hall at the bedroom we had been in.

"I like him. I really like him a lot, but we are just casual. Nothing serious. How about you and Theo?"

"I have no idea what's going on with us. Obviously, I don't know as much

about him as I thought I did." "Well, then it's settled. You will stay here

with me," Isabella said with a wide grin.

"I guess I could do that if Jack doesn't mind, of course."

"Oh, it was his suggestion when I told him we had been sleeping at the shelter."

"You did what?" I yelled as I stood up. "Oh, shit Isabella. He's going to tell Theo, and oh God …Why did you do that?"

"We were talking, and it just came out. I didn't want to lie to him."

Jack and Isabella seemed to have a pretty honest relationship. Jack was telling her about his escort business, Isabella was telling him about her and me staying at the shelter. It was clearly not the same kinds of conversations Theo and I'd had.

"It's fine Abby; he's not going to go blabbing to Theo."

"I can't take this, Isabella. I don't want to be involved with these guys anymore. Let's just go back to the way it was before."

"No. Absolutely not. This is a much better life than either of us could have imagined. You are just getting wrapped up in your emotions toward Theo. That's all there is to it. How about you look at this as an opportunity instead of some guy who has done something wrong to you. Theo is better looking and richer than most the guys you've gone out with in the past. Stop looking at it as something real, and just use him for what you can get."

The way she said it made me sound like the worst type of human being. Not only had I been using guys for their apartments, meals, etc. for the past few years, I hadn't even thought it was bad at all until that very moment. Only when the idea was combined with thoughts of Theo did I finally feel like I had been living my life very deceitfully.

"I can't do that to him," I said as we both looked at the door

as the lock was being unlocked. "Why not? You've done it

before."

"I like him," I said quickly before the door opened.

It was Jack, and Theo was right behind him. They had a bag full of what looked like Chinese food and both seemed really happy to see us. I felt myself light up at the sight of Theo before I remembered that I was mad at him.

"Abby, it's nice to see you," Jack said as he came over and kissed Isabella on the cheek. "And you, it's pretty fucking nice to see you too."

Isabella and Jack promptly started in on a make out session on the couch, so I got up to help Theo with the dinner. Neither of us said a thing as we took the food out of the boxes and put it onto everyone's plates. I wasn't sure if Jack had told him about where Isabella and I had been sleeping or if there was
another reason he was so quiet, but I wasn't about to be the first person to talk.

"So Theo, I hear you had some commotion at your restaurant today," Isabella said when she finally came up for air.

"Yes, I had to fire my manager and a waitress. But luckily, the assistant manager is a good guy, and I think he will work even better as the head guy out there."

"So you own a restaurant and run an escort business?" I asked, crossing my arms and staring at Theo.

His jaw dropped open as he looked at Isabella and Jack and then back toward me. I could tell he didn't know what to say, and he hadn't wanted me to know about it. He had that look on his face that every man got when their horrible secrets were finally revealed. I knew there had to be a fatal flaw in Theo. I knew he was too good to be true.

"It is one of my businesses, yes," he said without showing any emotion.

"So you guys picked us up to get us to work for you? Is that what this has all been?"

"Abby, I think you should cool down a bit," Isabella said as she pulled me toward her.

"I don't really feel like cooling down. I feel like someone telling me the truth. Did you pick me up because you wanted me to work for you as an escort? It's not a hard question. Yes or no?"

Theo looked at Jack and then back at me, but he still wasn't showing much emotion at all. I couldn't read him or what was going on in his mind. He no longer looked surprised by my confronting him. Instead, he just looked blankly at me.

"Yes, but …" he started to say before I interrupted him.

"Jack, is it alright if I stay here with you and Isabella?" I

said, turning my back to Theo. "Sure it is."

"Great, thank you. Did you know that Jack was honest with Isabella and told her everything? He didn't lie to her and pimp her out to his friends without her knowledge."

"Wait a minute. I didn't pimp you out at all. You made that deal with Aldo all on your own."

"I wouldn't have done it if I had known you two just liked tricking girls. I don't want to see you or Aldo ever again," I said, storming off toward the bedroom.

I felt myself shaking from the adrenaline of the moment, and then the tears came pretty quickly after that. I hated crying. It was my least favorite thing to do, and I didn't want anyone else to see me that emotional. But when Isabella came into the room, I instantly wrapped my arms around her neck and held onto her.

"I don't know why I'm so angry. I just hate that he lied to me. It hurts."

"It's because you like him, Abby. You've spent so much of the last few years pretending to have feelings for guys that you've forgotten what it's really like when you like a guy."

She was probably right, but I didn't want to like Theo at all. How could I have feelings for a guy that would outright lie to me? He wasn't a good guy, and I shouldn't have been having feelings for him at all.

"I don't want to like him. He's a liar," I said through my tears.

"Maybe you should give the guy a chance. You know Jack told me the truth because I told him the truth about my past. I didn't want to start anything with a lie and felt Jack was different. If you're going to be mad at Theo for lying, you should probably tell him the truth about yourself as well."

Oh, she had me on that one. But I wasn't ready to stop being mad at Theo for lying to me. Certainly, his lies were much worse than my lies of omission. I hadn't been trying to trick him or anything like that. I just didn't want him to know that I had been sleeping at the shelter or with other guys at their apartments for the last few years. It made me feel cheap and not like the person I really was.

"I didn't want to look like a cheap whore who was using people," I said.

"Well, maybe there was a reason Theo didn't want to tell you about his escort business? Maybe he didn't want you to think of him as a guy who ran an escort business?" Isabella said as she chuckled. "Perhaps you both lied to each other because you were both ashamed about your past? Maybe you could both forgive each other?"

I really hated when Isabella was right about things!

Chapter 8

THEO

"Shit, should I go in there?" I asked Jack as we both stood in the kitchen trying to figure out what to do.

"I wouldn't if I were you," Jack said with a smile. "So you actually like her? I'm confused; I thought we were supposed to be picking them up for the business."

Jack was right to be confused; I didn't normally find girls that I liked while we were out and certainly hadn't given him any warning that I actually liked her and might want to avoid telling her what I did for a living. I wasn't mad at Jack for telling the truth, I was angrier at myself for not telling the truth.

"I don't know what happened. Somewhere between picking her up and grooming her for the job, I started to think she was a pretty cool chick."

"Then what happened with Aldo? How did she end up going out with him?"

"I went over there to talk to him about that fiasco with Kimberly. I didn't want him getting pissed off that we had kicked the shit out of his guy. But when we got there, Aldo and Abby had met at her job or something, and he wanted to take her out. I couldn't exactly say no, I hadn't known her for more than twenty-four hours at that point."

"How is it that you have the ability to get yourself in so much trouble with the ladies all the time?" Jack laughed.

"Seriously, I'd like to fix this, but I'm not sure I can. Aldo wants to take her out again, and she's pissed off at me. Aldo will kill me if she doesn't agree to go out with him again."

"He's not going to kill you; come on, that guy loves you like you were his own son."

"No, you didn't hear him on the phone. He definitely will kill me or

at the very least, kick my ass." "Then go fix this."

"And just let her go out with him again? I don't even know if she will. She's pissed off at him also."

"If Aldo is really that angry at you, then you need to fix this. It's not worth going to jail over or losing everything just because of one girl. There's plenty more out there."

I hated the way Jack was talking, but I knew he was right. I wasn't going to be able to keep Abby with me if Aldo wanted her. There just was no way. As much as I genuinely liked her, I wasn't in any position to pull away from Aldo just yet. I was going to have to do some fast talking and try to mend things between the two of them.

Life wasn't about always getting my own way, and I knew that. But I particularly hated what I was about to do. I was going to have to push Abby toward Aldo, the one man that could destroy me.

I took a deep breath and made my way toward the room that Abby and Isabella were sitting in and
talking. I didn't like this at all, not one bit. I wanted to make up with Abby, but I didn't want her to make up with Aldo. I liked that she never wanted to go out with him or talk to him again; that made me really happy.

"Can I come in?" I asked after knocking on the door.

I could hear the girls in there talking, and they both stopped the second they heard my voice. Well, I thought they stopped until I leaned in closer and could tell they were whispering to each other. I'm sure Isabella had told Abby absolutely everything already so there was no point in lying to her. But I did need to make it clear that Aldo had nothing to do with it, and if she wanted to go out with him again, that she should. I absolutely hated myself for what I was about to do.

"Yes, you can come in," I heard Abby say.

"Sorry for interrupting, but could I talk with Abby for a minute?"

"Sure. I'll be right outside if you need anything," Isabella said as she looked at me with an evil eye.

I closed the door behind Isabella and crossed to the chair that was sitting next to the bed. I certainly wasn't going to sit on the bed with her after how angry she was. Plus, I had to give her up to Aldo and sitting near her was going to make that way too hard for me.

"What do you have to say? I'm ready to hear whatever excuse you can come up with. Perhaps another long list of lies? Give it to me," she said, crossing her arms.

Abby was angry, at least, I could tell when she was actually angry compared to when I thought she was angry. The look on her face was undeniable, and I wouldn't forget it anytime soon. I hated making her feel bad and wanted to wrap my arms around her and make everything better.

My whole life I had worked to make things better for people. I didn't start working with escorts because I thought it would make me a lot of money. When I first got into the business, it was to help out a couple of girls who had worked for Aldo and were struggling to find new clients. Aldo was phasing out his escort business and doing other illegal things for his side businesses, so it was the perfect opportunity to take over and help the girls out.

"I'm not going to lie to you, Abby. I'm here to straighten things out."

"Why did you even bother lying in the first place?" she said as she looked away from me. "I liked you, Theo; I wanted to get to know you. I even asked you what all that money was about and you lied right to my face."

"No. No, I didn't. I said we could talk about it later. I didn't lie."

Abby seemed more annoyed than ever at me when I said that so I decided it wasn't best to argue with her. That wasn't why I was there anyways; I needed to make her like Aldo again. The last thing I could handle was him coming after me.

"Well, I can see you're mad, and I don't want to upset you even more. I just wanted to straighten out one thing. Aldo, he didn't hire you as an escort. I had no idea he was going to make that offer to you and didn't tell him a thing about you. I certainly didn't tell him you were working for me."

"It doesn't matter. I don't want to see him again, and I certainly don't want to see you again."

"Abby," I said leaning forward. "Nothing was fake between us; the only reason I lied was because I thought you deserved better than a guy like me."

I was being more honest and real with Abby than I had been with any woman in a really long time. I hated that she felt like she didn't trust me and wanted her to feel safe around me. Honestly, I wanted to just turn off the rest of the world and climb into that bed with her until everything was perfect again.

"So you didn't think that I would understand what you did for a living and the logical explanation was to lie to me?"

"Yes, and look you certainly don't understand, and you're incredibly angry with me. Maybe I was right not to tell you the truth?"

"Oh, I'm not angry because you're an overpaid pimp! I'm angry because you lied to me!" she said raising her voice.

I had to disagree. She was angry at me for both lying to her and because I had a job that was far from ideal for any woman. No normal woman wanted to date a guy who set people up with escorts. I had learned this a long time before but had hoped to get away without telling Abby right away.

"There's no reason for you to raise your voice at me. I know you did some lying as well over the last few days."

"What? I have no idea what you are talking about," Abby said although she clearly had a guilty look on her face.

"You know damn well you don't live in those apartments I dropped you off at. You've got a storage unit at the building next door and slept at the shelter last night."

That was it, whatever I had said was the final straw, and Abby dropped any bit of decorum she had and got really pissed off. She stood up and started to pace the length of the bedroom while pondering what she wanted to say to me. Every time she started to speak, she would stop herself and then rethink what it was she wanted to say.

I waited with a high level of anticipation to see what it was that she was going to say to me. I just knew it was going to be something horrible or some explanation of how my lie was so much worse than the one she had told me.

"I'm sorry," she said as she walked up, wrapped her arms around me and hugged me.

It was the last thing I was expecting, and she totally caught me off guard. Why wasn't she still angry? Was she trying to trick me or something? Never in my life had a woman given up on an argument so quickly, particularly an argument that she was clearly winning.

"You're sorry?" I asked.

"Yes, I didn't want you to think I was using you, and I am so ashamed of not having a place of my own. I'm really sorry for lying," she said, holding on tight to me.

My plan was to get her to agree to go out with Aldo again. But as I held her in my arms, I knew for sure I wasn't going to be able to let her go. Gently, I grabbed her hair and pulled her face away from mine so I could look at her. Everything about her eyes was totally genuine, and I couldn't stop myself from kissing her.

The power between the two of us was too strong to resist, and the adrenaline from us fighting brought the intensity up a whole second notch. Every muscle in my body tried to resist Abby, but I just couldn't keep myself from holding onto her.

"Wait, we should stop," I whispered without a shred of truth in my words.

I didn't want to stop and knew damn well that Abby didn't want to stop either. Even if she was mad at me, I could feel every part of her body longing to be with me. I scooped her up and laid her on the bed as we both started frantically taking each other's clothes off.

Her soft hands on my body made me go into overdrive as my throbbing body ached to be inside of her. Normally, I could contain myself when I was with a woman. Typically, I could tease them, play with them, and make everything last for longer than imaginable. But this time, I couldn't stop myself; I had to be inside of her. I couldn't take it another moment.

"Condoms, we need condoms," Abby said, slightly out of breath.

At least, she was thinking the same thing I was thinking. But I knew Jack well, and he had condoms hidden in every corner of his apartment. I reached over for the nightstand and, sure enough, it had a wide variety of choices for us. I grabbed the first one my hand touched and ripped it opened. I was about to slide it on when Abby grabbed it from me and slowly rolled it down my shaft.

There was nothing better than having a sexy woman wrap your cock with a condom. Well, of course, there were things better ... just not in the realm of condom usage.

I let out a deep moan as her hands held onto me, but I couldn't wait any longer and ended up pushing her back onto the bed as I climbed between her thighs. The look of anticipation in her eyes was simply irresistible as I slid into her.

To control myself from exploding almost instantly, I had to think about something not related to the pleasure I was feeling there in that moment with Abby. My body moved slowly to try and control myself, but I just couldn't stand it. I had to feel the explosion.

Then Abby grabbed my back and pulled me toward her, giving me permission to thrust harder and harder. She wanted it just as much as I did and I felt that. Together, we moved quickly as one, and before I knew it, I felt myself exploding. The sweet release was so powerful that she screamed out in pleasure too as we both came at the same time.

It wasn't the best sex I'd had, and it certainly couldn't have been the best sex for Abby either. But we both needed that release, and it gave us permission to stop being angry with each other.

"I'm sorry I didn't tell you the whole truth," I said to her as I lay down next to her in the bed. "You deserve the truth. You deserve someone better than me."

Abby didn't say a thing, and instead just pulled her body close to mine. I wasn't used to a woman giving up on an argument as quickly as Abby had. It just wasn't familiar to me at all. Typically, women loved to argue, and even after I had thought something was settled, they continued to argue about it.

"I'm sorry too. I didn't want you to think I was using you or something like that. I really do like you, and I wanted you to like me and not feel sorry for me."

"I don't feel sorry for you," I said as I held her.

"Wait, not even a little bit?" she said as she sat up in bed with a huge smile. "I mean, I just admitted to being homeless; you should feel a little sorry for me," she teased.

"Okay, okay, maybe a little. But you're a smart girl; I can tell

you've got things figured out." "We should do that again,"

Abby said as she pushed me down and straddled me.

"Do that? Or something a little longer?" I asked with a smirk.

"Yeah, I could use a little longer. Maybe an inch or so,"

she said as she started to giggle. "What? No, you did not!"

I said as I grabbed her and started to tickle her.

"I did, and I don't even feel bad about it."

Never in my life had I ever felt bad about the size of my penis. I knew I was above average, and even her teasing didn't make me worry about it. But one thing I did like was how she was willing to forget our fight and have fun still. I liked Abby a lot, and it was going to be harder than ever to see her go on another date with Aldo. That was IF I could actually even convince her to do it. Now that she knew I was in the escort business, Abby might not consider going on a date with Aldo, no matter what I said.

"Come here," I said, pulling Abby down on top of me.

I almost let myself slide inside of her without a condom, but then reached to grab one. This time, I slid it on my cock without her help, and she quickly slid on top of me. She moaned as I entered her body but moved slowly and pressed me deep inside of her. It was nice to feel her tight muscles around me, and I couldn't wait to feel myself explode again.

But this time, she was in charge and moved slowly as her hips thrust back and forth on my hard body. My hands explored her ass and found just the right spot to grab hold of her and pull her harder against me.

With each thrust she made, I held her ass cheeks and urged her to go further. I couldn't stand it and soon felt myself thrusting against her as we moved together. Harder and longer I thrust as I worked to bring her to the climax of explosion.

I held out as long as I could so I could see her face as her body finally gave in to the pleasure. Soon, her body started to move faster, and I felt her muscles clench around me. Abby closed her eyes and her hands pressed hard into my chest as her hips grinded against me.

"Oh, fuck yes," she moaned as her clit rubbed against my body.

The stimulation from her thrusting and my cock inside of her was just what Abby needed to finally get the ultimate explosion. I watched intently as her body gave in to the pleasure that I had given her. There was nothing quite as wonderful as watching a woman have an orgasm.

"Oh ... oh ... oh, my, yes!" she screamed out as I held onto her body and pulled her down toward me so I could kiss her.

While our lips moved together, I let my body thrust inside of her so I could have my delightful ending. Her lips opened, and I felt her tongue slide into my mouth as my hips thrust upward as hard as they could. I held her ass tightly and over and over again thrust my cock into her until finally making one thrust that had me erupting.

"Fucking hell, what happened to us being

mad at each other." I laughed. "It was

makeup sex," she teased.

"We should definitely fight more often then." "Yes, like every single day. I'd like that."

I had no idea what was going on between the two of us. I certainly liked making love to her, but why
wasn't she angry at me? I had lied to her about my entire life, and she was perfectly fine with making love to me. She even joked about it being makeup sex. I really wanted to be able to let her go and push her toward Aldo but just couldn't stand the idea of it. I certainly couldn't stand the thought of him fucking her. That was an absolutely no, and I couldn't change my mind on that one.

Now my problem was huge, though. How was I going to appease Aldo now that I had Abby for myself? Certainly, he could understand that I wanted her. He wanted her just as badly, but he was married, and I wasn't. After all the years we had known each other, I thought for a moment that maybe Aldo would just let things be and let me be with Abby.

But then I remembered his words to me on the phone. He had threatened to kill me. He didn't threaten to beat me up and didn't threaten to injure me. Aldo had been very clear about his threat and had threatened to kill me. Certainly, I wasn't going to be able to convince him to change his mind.

Whatever I decided to do, I couldn't give up Abby. As I wrapped her in my arms and pulled the covers up over us, the one thing I knew for certain was that I couldn't give her up.

Chapter 9

ABBY

In the span of one evening, we had gone from arguing and I totally didn't want to see him again to making love and cuddling. I had to laugh a little at that moment. But despite knowing that Theo had lied to me, I couldn't stand the idea of staying mad at him. Then when he brought up knowing that I had stayed at the shelter, it just made me realize that he was really a good guy. I knew more than anyone that sometimes you lied to people you cared about.

I had been lying to my sisters for years. Every time I'd call them, I would tell them how well things were going. I would lie and say I had extra money that I was sending back to them when the reality was that I had no money at all. It was like I would rather know that they were going to eat and be able to pay their heating bill than if I had food the next day.

When I worked at the restaurant, I knew I would always have at least one meal there. Plus, I could sneak food from dishes that they were going to throw away, and I always had plenty of bread. But the days I worked at the dance club only, well, sometimes on those days I just had lots of olives from the bar or sometimes a protein bar from one of the other girls.

Lying was sometimes a necessity, and I knew that. I couldn't fault Theo for doing the exact same thing I had been doing for years.

It was weird that I felt so comfortable with Theo, and that was another reason I was so willing to forgive him. I just didn't feel like he was judging me at all. When we were together in that room, it felt like I could have said I was an ax murderer and he would have still wanted to be with me. Not that I would ever murder anyone, but it was reassuring to know that the man you were with would still love you if you did.

"Good morning," I whispered, pulling Theo's arms tighter around me. "I'm still dreaming," he said.

"Nope you're here, with J-Lo, this isn't a dream," I joked. His hand slid down to my bare ass, and he squeezed it.

"I think this is Abby; J Lo doesn't have a sweet ass like this."

Theo lightly slapped my ass and then let his hand slide around and cup one of my breasts as he kissed the back of my neck. I wasn't normally a cuddlier, but it actually felt comfortable there with Theo.
Everything felt different with Theo. I had to assume that's what it was like when people actually had feelings for the man they slept in the same bed with.

"Do you want some breakfast?" I asked, starting to sit up.

Theo held onto me and wouldn't let me go. He wrapped his arms even tighter and pulled me close to him.

"I need to tell you something. I hope you'll understand and hope you won't hate me."

The tone of his voice was not reassuring, and I pushed away from him and sat up in bed to prepare myself for what he was going to tell me. How much worse could it be than the fact that he ran an escort business?

"Please don't tell me you're also a drug dealer? You actually said that you weren't right to my face." "No. God, I hate that stuff. No, it's about Aldo. I need you to go out with him again if he calls you."

"Why on earth would you want me to go out with him again? I thought things were good with us? Wait, do you actually want me to be an escort?"

I wasn't mad at the moment, but I really didn't understand what was going on. He said he didn't want me to be an escort, and now there he was telling me to go out with Aldo again. I didn't even know if Aldo would ask me out again. It seemed like he really wasn't all that interested in me when our date ended.

"I'm going to tell you the truth. I mean all of it. The only reason I'm telling you is because I care about you and want you to hang around. Do you understand?"

Theo was starting to scare me a little. His voice was so serious that I felt like he was talking about something deadly, not another date with an attractive, respectful older man. And the truth was, I would go out with Aldo again if it was alright with Theo; $10,000 went a long way to helping my sisters, and Aldo didn't try to have sex with me or anything like that. I still didn't know what had changed toward the end of the night, but overall it was a good night.

"I can handle the truth much better than I handle lies," I said with a sweet smile, grabbing his hand.

"When I first came to New York, I ran into Aldo, and he offered to help me business. But I absolutely did not intend for him to take you out. I only wanted to date you for myself. I've been working to get out of the escort business and build up my legitimate world. I thought, possibly, I could avoid telling you the truth while I did that. I'm sorry about that."

"OK, so you're saying he just asked me out because he wanted to?"

I didn't really understand what Theo was trying to get at. Was Aldo in charge of the business or something? Did Theo let Aldo make his decisions for him? But I did like hearing that Theo wanted to get out of the business. It was certainly something that made me happy. Obviously, we hardly knew each other, but if things were ever going to move forward, I didn't want to have any involvement in his escort business. It did make a lot more sense why there were so many women handing him envelopes full of money.

"He asked you out because he could tell it bothered me when he was talking about you. When the two of us went to the back room, I told him you weren't going to work for me and not to mess with you. But when you said you had family back home, he couldn't resist. He knew I wouldn't refuse him."

"That's fine, so I won't go out with him anymore. Problem solved."

"No. Actually, I really need you to say yes if he asks you out again. I can't afford to have him pissed off at me. Apparently, something happened on your date that he thinks is my fault."

I had to think for a minute as I tried to figure out what that could possibly be Theo's fault. Nothing had happened at all that would make Aldo think about Theo; I really couldn't think of a thing. The only thing that happened was I kissed Aldo, and we talked to one last client, then Aldo decided he wanted to take me home. He switched how he dealt with me after the kiss. But I couldn't see how that would be Theo's fault.

"I can't think of much that really happened. What does he think is your fault?"

"I'm not sure. Please don't get mad at me when I ask you this, and I absolutely know it's none of my business, but did you sleep with him?"

I had to laugh. I was naked in bed with Theo, and he was asking me if I slept with Aldo, and he actually expected that I would answer him. But the look on his face was serious, and I felt compelled to answer him.

"No, I didn't sleep with him. I did kiss him, though." "You kissed him? He

didn't initiate it?"

"Yep."

"Ah, that's what it was then. He thinks I told you about the whole escort thing and that that was your first job. He has a thing for unwilling women, and you kissing him made him think you were more than willing, or you knew about the escort business."

"I'm so confused. So he wants to help you with new girls, but he doesn't want them to know what they are getting into?"

"He's the typical dirty old man. He likes the naive girl who he can teach everything. If you kissed him, then he probably thought you were well versed in the escort world."

"All from a kiss?"

"He likes to be denied what he wants, and usually, young naïve girls will do that. You threw him off his game with the kiss."

It was weird to be sitting there talking with Theo about my kiss with Aldo. But it was freakishly
comfortable. Again, I didn't feel judged at all by Theo for kissing Aldo. I felt safe talking to him, and I liked that.

"So what do you want me to do? You want me to go out with him?"

"Yes, if he asks you out again, I'd love it if you'd say yes. Of course, you keep all of the money, and it would be a business deal between the two of you. I definitely don't want to be involved in it."

"So you don't want to come and have a threesome," I joked.

"You're such a troublemaker," Theo said as he grabbed me and pulled me back down on the bed. "I'm
really trying to get away from him, but he holds so much power. I've got to figure out a way to break free without getting myself killed."

"Wait a minute? Aldo would kill you? I don't think so. He seems like a pretty cool guy."

"Abby, he's killed more people in the last year than I have my entire life," Theo said and my eyes opened wider than I ever thought possible.

"You've killed someone?" I said, sitting back up and looking at him. "With your hands? Or did you shoot them? Did you mean to kill them?"

Theo laughed at first, and I could tell he was trying to decide if he wanted to tell me the story that was on the tip of his tongue.

"I killed a guy once a long time ago in a fight. But he was going to kill me if

I hadn't killed him first." "Wow, I slept with a killer, that's pretty freaky," I

said, plopping my head onto the pillow next to him.

The funny thing was, I didn't really care at all that Theo had killed someone. It seemed normal to me in my jaded mind. I had seen so much while in New York the last few years; nothing really phased me much at all anymore.

"Yep, I'm a killer and so is Aldo; so you be careful and don't make him mad."

"Why shouldn't I just blow him off? Certainly he's a grownup who can take no for an answer."

"No, he's not able to take no for an answer. Except when flirting. He likes it when you tease him, flirt with him, get him all worked up and then deny him. That turns him on. But it's a balance, and you can't actually say the word no to him."

"This is so complicated."

"I know it is, but you're good at this back and forth game. I know you can handle him. I've got to get my affairs in order with my restaurant and my gym before I try and cut off ties with Aldo."

"So you want me to help you get away from Aldo. Does that mean you're going to give up the escort world? It seems like that's a lot of money. Why would you want to give that up?"

I saw the look of confusion on Theo's face at my question. Of course, I didn't like the idea of the escort business for myself and wasn't even that fond of going out on a date with a guy that ran such a business. But I was a realist and knew that money like Theo had must have come from his escort business. Unless he really was a whiz at investing, but I doubted it based on the new recollection of his illegal business.

"Um, you want me to keep doing it?" he asked with a bewildered expression.

"I'm not saying you should or shouldn't keep doing it. But from the amount of cash I have seen women handing you over the past few days, it seems like a lucrative enterprise. Why would you want to stop?"

I knew in my mind why someone would want to stop, but I really was interested in seeing what Theo had to say. Turning over a new leaf wasn't easy, in fact, most the people I knew who said they were going to change, never did. Perhaps Theo was just really good at persuading people, and this was all just a lie to get me into the business; I had no idea for sure, but my eyes were open now at least, and that made it much easier for me to move forward with whatever was going on between Theo and me.

"It's illegal. I will never be able to find a nice woman and settle down while

I'm in this business." "You found me."

"But I had to lie to you right away. I don't want to worry about getting arrested and going to jail. It's a stressful life. Plus, look what happened to Kimberly. I'm tired of dealing with jackholes like that."

Theo's life was starting to look more and more like a soap opera to me. But at least, it was all making sense. Kimberly worked for him as an escort, that's why he felt bad for what happened to her and had her at his house. At least, Theo had a conscience.

"I need some time to think about all of this. I don't know if I'm up for it. Maybe I am, but maybe I'm not. Do you mind if I take some time?"

"Sure, but let me know if Aldo contacts you. Or if you don't want to talk to me about it, that's fine. Just don't tell him that you know about the whole escort thing."

I didn't like the idea of lying to Aldo, but I also didn't like the idea of a guy as deadly as Aldo being
angry at me. Surely it wouldn't matter too much if I just went along with the innocent thing for awhile. Before I knew everything that Theo had told me, I really did like Aldo. Perhaps it was the dangerous side of him that made me drawn to him. I wasn't sure, but for the time being, I would go along with it. Aldo had no reason to be angry at me or try to kill me, so I felt relatively safe around him.

"I'll keep in touch with you. I'm going to stay here with Isabella and Jack,

though, if you don't mind." "Yes, I think that's a great idea."

We were both still naked in the bed and things were getting a little awkward now. I wanted to keep
talking to him, but I also didn't want to keep talking to him. He had unloaded a ton of information on me, and it was highly likely that I was going to need to take some notes if I wanted to keep everything straight.

"I'm going to hop in the shower. I'll call you if I hear from Aldo," I said as I got out of the bed and walked naked to the shower.

"Do you want some company?" "Not today," I said with a smile.

I really did want him to come in the shower with me, but it didn't seem like the right time. The strange thing about spending time with Theo was that I always wanted to spend more time with him. He drove me crazy, made me angry, stirred up all kinds of emotions inside of me, yet I still wanted him there with me.

If this was what went on for women in relationships, I was glad I had skipped out on most of that throughout my life. My stomach was in knots as I thought about all the information that Theo had given me and everything I now knew about him.

When I had first met him, he was like a celebrity to me with all his money and his plane. I idolized him as we went to Las Vegas and he bought me everything my heart desired. I couldn't understand why he didn't want to be with me more on the trip; I still didn't know why he hadn't joined me in the shower of our luxury room in Las Vegas. But what I was certain of more than I had been before, Theo was just a normal guy with some extraordinary problems in his life. He was just like the rest of us; trying to make lemonade out of the lemons life handed him.
with my business. I was naive at the time and didn't really know what the long-term effects of my decisions were. So I agreed to let Aldo loan me some money so I could start my business."

"Your escort business?"

"Yes, it's a good business, and I know it sounds horrible, but I can tell you more about it if you'd like. It's really not so bad."

"Finish the story about Aldo."

"So over the years, I have let him go out with girls that I wanted to work for me. He would take them out and help me decide if I should invite them into the

Chapter 10

THEO

Life sure had a way of twisting things around and making them as difficult as possible. When Abby walked into my life, I had quickly gone from a guy who was thinking of getting out of the business, to a guy who needed a plan to get out right away. There was no time to wait, and I had to figure things out quickly. I really wasn't sure how Aldo was going to react when he heard I really wanted out.

Sure, he knew I had been considering it. But I think he always expected I would stay in the business a little bit, perhaps like he had. To him, getting out of the business simply meant that you didn't do the front end stuff anymore, but you still got the money from the work that everyone else was doing. That wasn't what I wanted to do; I wanted out totally. If Jack wanted to keep the business up, he could buy it from me. But I wasn't going to take a monthly stipend from him and wasn't going to be involved at all. I really wanted out.

"Good morning to you," Isabella said as I walked out into Jack's living room. "Someone got lucky last night."

Isabella was more like the typical woman I dealt with. She had attitude and nothing really phased her. I could see why she and Abby had gotten together. Abby was quiet, and Isabella was boisterous. Abby seemed like she was shy, and Isabella seemed like she could talk to anyone at any time. Isabella also seemed much more street smart than Abby; Isabella was the typical woman I recruited to be an escort. Abby was not the typical escort, but that's why she would make so much money in the business if I had recruited her. Abby's ability to be real with people set her apart from girls like Isabella.

"Morning Isabella, how are things with you?"

"Things … they are good. I really like your friend, Jack. He's a cool dude."

"From what I hear, he likes you too and thinks you're a groovy chic."

"Psychedelic."

"Now, why exactly are we talking like we are in the seventies?" I asked, grabbing a cup of coffee. "No reason, I just like to add color to my vocabulary every now and then."

"Okay then. Where's Jack at?" "I think he went for a run."

"What? Are you sure?"

"Yeah, he said he wanted to start working out and getting into shape," Isabella said as we sat at the table.

I had known Jack for a long time and working out wasn't really his thing. He liked to party, drink and pick up women. But I figured there was a first time for everything, and I was living proof of that.

"So what's up with the two of you? Are you a thing?"

"I guess a thing is the best way to describe us," she joked. "How about you and Abby, did you two make up?"

"I think we did. Sort of, at least. I'm pretty sure she's going to stay here and not at my house, but that's better than hating me; right?"

"It's surprising that she actually forgave you. She does tend to hold some pretty intense grudges. But Abby's a good girl, Theo; she's not meant for this kind of business. Please don't drag her into it."

"That's what my hope is in all of this. I don't want her in the business, and I'm not going to stay in it much longer either. I think it's time to move on with real life."

"Now that sounds like the kind of man I can support dating my friend."

"Speaking of real life, I need to head to my gym and straighten some things out. Tell Abby I'll call her later, and when you see Jack, tell him to stop by my gym if he's getting into the working out thing. I'll set him up with a trainer so he can do it right."

"Sounds good. Have fun in the real world."

"Have fun here, I guess," I said as I grabbed my things and left Jack's house.

Jack was a ladies' man that was for certain, but I liked Isabella, and she seemed to be someone who would fit well with Jack in the long run. She was street smart, laid back and funny; perfect for Jack. I wondered if Isabella was going to start doing escort work or not but decided not to ask her. I wanted out of the business, and that meant I was going to let Jack deal with as much of the day to day work as possible for the time being.

The top floor of Merck Towers was the perfect place for my gym, but it also cost millions of dollars per month to keep that spot. To make a profit, we were going to have to start taking in much bigger names, and I was probably going to have to hire some more trainers. Luckily, I already had an amazing manager for the gym, so I didn't have to worry about that aspect of the business.

When the elevator opened, I took in the view of the city, like I did every time I visited my gym. It was simply awe-inspiring to see the entire skyline from that floor. We even had a deck you could go out on and workout equipment out there as well. My gym was my dream long before the restaurant, and I paid much more attention to the numbers behind the gym. Unfortunately, I was losing about a million dollars each month in that business and hadn't put in the time or effort to figure out how to make it profitable.
Certainly, there had to be something I could change to quickly make a profit and turn my money pit into a way of actually surviving.

With a name like Sunrise Sanders you would have expected to see my gym manager on a stripper pole somewhere instead of behind a desk. Sunrise was a vibrant woman who had hippy parents and no real structure growing up; so she compensated by keeping her entire life as structured as possible.

"Ms. Sanders, how's the gym doing?" I asked as I knocked on her office door.

"Things are great. We have a steady increase in clients and some interest from a few celebrity trainers." "Tell me more."

"About the trainers?" "Yes."

"Well, one of them has a reality show and wants to bring camera crews here. I wasn't sure about the legalities of that since we have other clients and other trainers so I said we would talk about it and get back to them. The other trainer works primarily with celebrities, but he wanted to know about the safety of our balcony."

"Why? That seems like a weird thing to worry about," I asked as Sunrise handed me the accounting books from the last month.

"Apparently, one of his celebrity clients has bipolar disorder, and he didn't like how easy it would be for her to jump over the ledge."

"Oh, Jesus. No, I can't have a client like that around here. That would ruin us for sure if someone committed suicide from our club."

"That's what I thought at first too, but he is willing to pay a premium fee, and with him here we will get some other high name trainers from the city. I agreed to look into the cost of some sort of fencing or safety mesh or something."

That was exactly why I loved working with Sunrise, she knew we needed the money, but she also knew we couldn't afford to have anyone committing suicide from our building. I trusted her implicitly with the gym.

"Good idea, but I don't want something that's going to ruin the view for everyone. Maybe we could do a Plexiglas extension of two feet up? That should be a good deterrent, and it won't impede on the view at all."

"I'll see what I can find. Is there anything else you wanted updating on?"

I had come in prepared to ask a ton of questions, but most of them had been answered before I could even ask them. I looked through the books from the last month and tried to pretend I knew what I was looking at. Certainly I knew the basics but could never really tell if things were going well or not. It was like looking at a foreign language; even if I understood a little bit of what I saw, I couldn't understand everything.

"I really want to start building things here. I think we have the groundwork set pretty well, so it's time to grow. Is there anything you need to make that happen?"

I saw the instant surprise on Sunrise's face at the notion that I wanted to grow things. Normally, I just looked at the books and didn't have much else to offer. But I needed this company to do well, and that meant I was going to be more involved. Because the alternative was letting Aldo continue to control my life, and I couldn't do that. I already felt horrible that Abby was going to have to go out with him again. I needed to do my part to get out of the escort business.

"Oh, my God, I have so many ideas," Sunrise said, pulling out a notebook that she had tons of scribbles in. "I've been taking notes and preparing for this day. Oh, gosh, there are so many things," she said as she flipped through the notebook.

"How about you decide what you think are the number one and number two items on your list, and we can talk about those things first?"

Sunrise continued to flip through her notebook in a never-ending effort to find the notes she was looking for. It was actually quite exciting to see that she was so eager to help the company grow. I hoped she would remain that eager.

"Okay, okay, first of all we need to advertise. But not in regular newspapers or anything like that. We need a full page add in the Robb Report, do you know that magazine?"

"Yes, but are you sure that would be best? Isn't that more for people who don't live in the city?"

"Yes and no. But here is the second thing, and it will all tie in together. I think we should offer a monthly membership that includes personal training. That way people who are not already connected with a trainer could come in and workout with whoever is here. Of course, we will have to talk it over with the trainers and give them a cut, but it would be a more manageable amount each month because the trainers would just cover certain times but might be working with more than one client during those times. It will also help the trainers to gain new clients too. Because if someone likes one particular trainer, they could sign up for time with them at a discounted price. Does that make sense?"

It actually did make sense to me and sounded like a great idea. I even thought our trainers would enjoy the idea. Anything that would help bring in more money for them as well as increase their brand would be helpful.

"Go ahead and put together a proposal for me and I'll talk with the trainers next week. Set up an all staff meeting for me."

"Oh, man this is epic. This gym is going to be insane!" Sunrise said as she stood up and started pacing the room.

Her energy couldn't be contained, and I didn't feel like watching her pace the room so I said my goodbyes and went out to the balcony. It was going to be weird to have a safety wall out there, but it was probably a good idea, even if we didn't have that new mentally ill client. The wall we had now was regulation, but I still found people trying to lean over and look at the ground sometimes. I had been scared plenty of times that something bad would happen.

When my phone rang, I grabbed a chair and pulled up to the edge of the balcony so I could enjoy the view. It was Aldo again, and I expected he was still angry and I was going to have to do some sweet talking to calm him down.

"So what's the story?" Aldo asked. "Aldo, what? I told you already."

"I just called her, and she is going to help me look at apartments and go to dinner with Briggs. Everything is good on your part?"

My stomach instantly felt like releasing all the contents from my breakfast. Briggs was one of Aldo's friends that wasn't very nice to the girls at all. He liked to get rough with them, and sometimes things got out of control. Briggs tried not to leave marks and never meant to hurt the girls, he just liked it when they fought back. He was certainly not going out with Abby, and I was going to make sure of that.

"Aldo, she's not interested in being an escort. There really is no need for you to take her out. She's just a sweet girl from Kansas that I picked up in a club."

"Since when did you go so soft? She's the perfect escort and will make us tons of money. I'm moving forward with grooming her. She might take a little longer than others, but she's got the chops for it."

"Aldo, I like this girl. I like her so much I've been thinking of getting out of the business for real and trying things with her."

Aldo was silent, and that was a bad sign. It was a risk telling Aldo that I actually liked Abby. He could decide to help me out or he could decide he was going to take her out anyways despite my feelings.

"This is the problem with you young guys, you live in a fairytale world where women can love you for more than just your money. I'm doing you a favor by taking her off your hands. She would have just
caused you heartache."

"Aldo, come on man. You know me, I don't get all sappy with the girls, but this one is different."

Abby was different, and so was I. The time had come to get out of the business, and it was going to be a bit messy if Aldo didn't decide to just cut me loose. I wasn't exactly sure how messy things were going to get, but I was ready to get out now. My mind was made up, and when I made my mind up, that was all there was to it.

"I don't give a fuck if you like her or not. This girl is money, and I'm not about to give up money so you can play house. I'm also not about to let a good business go up in smoke. You can step back a little if you want to, but you're not closing up shop. Let's remember that I made you. It was my money that gave you your start. If it wasn't for me, you wouldn't have a goddamn thing!"

I knew at that moment that things were going to get ugly if I really wanted to get out. For as much as Aldo talked about going straight, he wanted to make it look like he went straight while everyone else around him was doing all the dirty work.

"Aldo, I'm sorry, but my life is mine now. I'll be happy to pay you a million dollars to offset your losses from me for the next year or so. Would that work?"

"Who the fuck do you think you are? You think you can just decide when you're going to cut me off? It doesn't work that way kid."

I could tell by the tone of his voice that Aldo didn't want to talk about it anymore, and I certainly wasn't going to keep pissing him off. If I was going to get out of the business, it wasn't going to happen by just asking him. That was clearly obvious.

"I'm sorry, Aldo. It was just something I was thinking about. You're right; it is probably best to just stay put for a while. Maybe somewhere done the road, we can talk about it."

"Just remember who made you, Theo. This isn't some game. I'll take you out as quickly as I brought you into this."

"Yes, I understand."

I wanted to ask more about Abby, but I figured it wasn't the best time to push him on that. It was going to be best for me just to tell Abby not to go out with him. He would get much less angry at her if she decided she didn't want to see him. Certainly, he would be pissed off still, but at least, no one would be getting murdered.

"Let's not have this conversation again anytime soon." "Okay," I said just as

Aldo hung up the phone.

I quickly dialed Abby's number, but it just rang and rang without an answer.

I hung up and dialed Jack. "Jack, is Abby still there?"

"No man, she and Isabella went out. What's up?"

"I need to get hold of her, do you know where they went?"

"Not sure, they were too busy with all their girl talk to tell me. Do you want me to call Isabella?"

"Yeah, if you get hold of her, please have Abby call me. I have to talk to her

before Aldo gets to her." "It sounds serious."

"Jack, if I left the business, would you want to take over?" "You're leaving?"

"No, I mean it's just an idea. I'm just throwing it around," I said, trying to downplay the idea. "No man, I wouldn't want to do it without you."

"Alright man, I'll let you know. For now, please try to call Isabella," I said as I hung up the phone. I had to find Abby and talk to her before she agreed to see Aldo again.

Chapter 11

ABBY

"Hi, Aldo, how are you?" I asked when he called me.

I knew I needed to be nice to him for Theo's sake, but I didn't really mind. Aldo had been really nice to me, and I thought the evening had gone really well up until I kissed him and ruined it.

It was exciting to me out with Aldo; I suspected it would feel even more dangerous now that I knew more about him. A smart girl would have been afraid to go out with Aldo, but I guess I wasn't so smart after all because I was excited to see him again. The dark mystery was appealing to me. It was also appealing to feel the way I did around him. Aldo had a command about him that was unlike any man I had ever been with. It was much clearer to me now after talking with Theo; Aldo was like that with everyone.

"I'm going to send a car for you at five o'clock," Aldo said

without answering my question. "Okay, where should I

wait?"

"You can stay where you are. He can come get you there, just give me the address."

Isabella and I were standing outside the women's shelter talking with some of our friends. It certainly
wasn't the best spot to have Aldo come and pick me up. But I couldn't think of another place quickly, so I had to wing it.

"He can pick me up at the women's shelter; I'm volunteering there today," I said, shrugging my shoulders at the women around me.

Everyone that was around me knew that I wasn't volunteering at the shelter. On the nights that I slept there, it was certainly a good enough place for me, but it wasn't someplace I wanted to hang out and volunteer at if I didn't have to. I did fantasize about being rich enough to bring a huge stack of new blankets to the shelter someday. The blankets that were there were disgusting.

"The shelter?" Aldo asked, and I hoped he wouldn't keep asking me questions. It was incredibly hard to lie to Aldo.

"Yes, the women's shelter on fifty-second."

"I know where it is," Aldo said slightly annoyed. "He will be there at five. You'll need to dress nice. We are going to look at an apartment my friend is selling, and then we will likely go to dinner."

"I can change, no worries. I'm excited to see you again," I said in as upbeat sounding voice as I could muster up.

Something seemed different with Aldo, but I couldn't quite put my finger on what it was. He was still nice to me, and I was excited to see him again, but things felt different between us.

It probably didn't help that I had Theo on my mind and wished I was spending the night with him, instead.

"See you at five, dear."

And just like that he was off the phone. I wondered how his wife dealt with him always being so serious. Perhaps he had a different side that only she knew. Maybe when they were alone, he was super funny. I could only imagine what their life was like together in their open relationship. It certainly was an odd thing for me to understand. But then again, if I was married to someone as serious as Aldo, I might be interested in finding a little fun on the side.

I did wonder if the whole story was true, though. I couldn't imagine a woman that was married to Aldo would be willing to sleep around on him. Unless, maybe she only slept with other women? Aldo had said she liked me. That made much more sense to me than the idea of her sleeping with other men. Perhaps if the topic came up during our evening, I would ask him. I snickered to myself; there was no way I was going to ask him anything that personal.

"I'm going out with Aldo at five o'clock," I said to Isabella and our friends.

"Shit, we need to fix you up. Let's go grab one of those dresses Theo gave you out of the storage unit," Isabella said as she started walking and didn't even wait for me.

"Wait, I told him to

pick me up here at five

o'clock." "Then we

better hurry."

Isabella walked like she had someone chasing her. I literally had to jog just to keep up with her. It was funny to see Isabella so involved in who I was going out with. I could tell that the excitement of everything I had told her was getting to her. She was the one who normally dated exciting people, and I was the one who normally dated boring people. It was fun to have someone exciting to go out with. Both Theo and Aldo were exciting to me.

Theo was certainly much more of my dream guy. Even with everything that had gone on between us, I
could tell that he was a good guy and that we would do well together. Of course, I didn't like that he had set me up with Aldo. Or that he hadn't refused to let me go out with him. That part of everything was hard for me to understand.

On the other hand, I enjoyed my time with Aldo. He was unlike any man I had been with, and I fantasized about being with him. I would never admit it to Theo, but if the moment came up for me to sleep with Aldo, I thought I might do it. He wasn't a normal boring guy, that was for sure, and I couldn't help imagining what it would be like to make love to him.

I imagined that Aldo was a gentle lover. Perhaps he took time to make his woman happy before he moved on to his own happiness. Especially after learning that he liked delayed gratification; all I could think about was how he would probably want to give his woman multiple orgasms while he tortured himself by not giving in.

"Abby, are you listening to me?" Isabella said as I finally came out of my daze and actually started listening to her.

"Of course."

"Then what did I say?"

"I have no idea," I said as we both started laughing.

"This one is the sexiest, but this one is the prettiest; which one do you want to wear?" Isabella asked as she held up two of the dresses that Theo had purchased for me.

"That one for sure," I said, pointing to the sexiest one.

It had a low cut back, and I was dying to feel Aldo's hand on my back again. Certainly, I was comforted in the fact that all he wanted to do was tease himself with my body. That suddenly made it much easier for me to tease him back. On our first date, I thought all about not being too sexy because I didn't want him to expect sex from me. But if he really didn't want sex, then I was going to turn on the sex appeal.

"How much is Aldo paying you for today's fun?"

"Oh, crap, I didn't even ask him. Maybe I'm just going out with him for free. Like a normal girl instead of an escort."

"Speaking of escorts, I've got my first date tonight. I didn't want to tell you; I wanted to surprise you when I was done. But I can't keep it inside any longer."

"You're really going through with it? How do you know the guy is safe? Did I tell you about what happened with that girl at Theo's house? There are some crazy people out there."

Isabella always had a much bigger sense of adventure than I did, so it wasn't unusual that she wasn't worried at all. In fact, it would have been more unusual if she had been worried about going out with a stranger.

"It's alright. Jack knows the guy, and he's a good high roller."

I absolutely hated that Isabella was so excited to be an escort, but I was pretty much doing the same thing, so I didn't have anything really to say. As much as I didn't want to consider what I was doing with Aldo as the same thing an escort would do, I knew it was. I knew that by agreeing to go out with him for money, I had taken a big step into a world that I wasn't really sure I wanted to be part of.

"You be safe out there," I said to Isabella.

It was the same thing we always said to each other at the end of the night when we went home with someone. Especially if we felt a little concerned about the person the other was going home with.

"You be safe out there with your super handsome older rich man," she teased me.

Exactly at five o'clock, a black SUV pulled up to the shelter. A nice guy got out and opened the door for me. He didn't say a word to me and didn't offer an introduction at all. It seemed a little clandestine for my taste, but I figured I should just go with it, knowing Aldo was sending the car for me.

When we pulled in front of Trump Towers, I was pretty damn excited. I had secretly always wanted to see inside that place. Aldo was just inside the front door, and he quickly opened it for me when I arrived. He was an old school gentleman and that was admirable to me. There weren't that many men out there that truly still treated women with dignity and respect.

"Good evening Miss Abigail, you look ravishing," he said with a slight smile.
"Thank you, sir," I said playfully.

I knew I looked damn good in my dress and hoped Aldo was going to pay me again for spending the evening with him. Even though we hadn't discussed money at all during our call, we had discussed it before, so I assumed he was going to give me another $10,000. Unfortunately, I knew that assuming something didn't make it true.

"We are going to meet my friend Briggs Moeller here. He's a real estate agent and has a penthouse for sale that he wants to show me."

"The penthouse is here? In Trump Towers?" "Yes, of course."

"I'm so excited," I said as I latched onto his arm and walked with him into the building.

I could tell instantly that Aldo liked it when I grabbed onto him. He liked the playful excitement I showed, and I made a mental note to keep doing it. I had started to understand the role of an escort, even though I hated that

that was what I was. As an escort, it wasn't my job to be there with the man, it was my job to make him feel like he wanted to feel while I was there. My little conversation with Theo had certainly, helped me a lot in figuring out what Aldo liked, and I couldn't

wait to test my skills on him. "Did I tell you how amazing you look?"

Aldo asked when we entered the elevator.

I liked that he seemed more like himself than he had seemed on the phone. Over the phone, he had sort of sounded annoyed with me, and I was concerned he wasn't going to be fun at all when I saw him that night.

"I picked this dress just for you. Look at the back," I said as I rapidly twisted around to show Aldo the plunging back of my dress.

He quickly pinned me against the wall as he came up behind me. His five o'clock shadow on his face pressed up against my back as his lips gently kissed my exposed skin. I was so turned on that it made me feel guilty almost instantly. I didn't want to be there with Aldo, and I was only doing it because I knew it would help Theo and because Theo said that Aldo liked the tease more than the actual action. But I felt guilty because I was so damn turned on by Aldo.

"You wore this for me?"

"Yes," I said as I pressed my ass back toward him. "You wanted to tease

me?" he questioned.

"No, I wanted to please you," I said innocently.

Aldo quickly twisted me around as he continued to press up against me. I felt his intense stare as he looked from my lips up to my eyes. I knew I had to hold his eye contact, but his intensity was too much for me, and I eventually looked to the ground.

"What else do you want to do to please me?" he asked in an aggressive tone.

I knew what he meant. He was trying to see if I knew about the whole escort thing or not. This was my time to prove it to him, to prove to Theo too, I had the acting skills that I needed for this part. Even though I was horrible at lying to someone, I had always wanted to be an actress, and that meant that I needed to use those skills at that moment.

"I don't know," I said shyly as I looked up at him. "I like the feeling of having you near me." "So if I wanted to fuck you right here in the elevator, that would be fine?" Aldo asked.

"No!" I said as I pressed him away. "And I didn't think you were that kind of guy."

I looked angrily at him and crossed my arms in front of him. I had to pretend to be offended by the offer. My job was to convince Aldo that I wouldn't sleep with him just because he had paid me money. It was a silly game, but I was more than happy to play that game if it meant I could help Theo and that I didn't have to actually sleep with Aldo.

"I'm sorry, that was a joke. Of course, you deserve better than an elevator," Aldo said as he pulled my hand from in front of me and held onto it. "Let's enjoy the apartment showing. You can tell me if it's a place a woman like you would want to live in."

"Well, I'd like to live pretty much in any apartment here. So we can save you time," I teased. "Let's get back to you kissing my back. I liked that use of our time much better."

Aldo smiled back at me, but we kept walking toward the apartment. When we arrived, Aldo didn't knock or anything, and instead, we went right inside. A tall man was inside; he was dressed in an expensive suit, but he looked like a jerk. The way he held himself slightly cocked to the side and his slick hair were not appealing to me at all. He was probably similar in age to Aldo, but certainly I did not have the same attraction to him.

The two men said hello, and then Briggs gave us a tour of the large two-story penthouse condo. It was exciting to see such an amazing place, but I didn't actually like it at all. I especially didn't like it when Briggs said the cost was over $30 million. It was old and outdated and seemed like it would need to be totally renovated before anyone would want to live in it. And for that price, you could certainly buy a brand-new condo on another block.

Aldo got a phone call and left me there with Briggs. It was awkward between us, and I instantly felt like this was some sort of test again. Briggs

moved up close to me and started to trace his hand down my chest. It was so incredibly rude that I couldn't stop myself from reacting. "Excuse me," I said sternly. "What do you think you're doing?"
"Just getting a little taste of the merchandise," he said with a cheesy car salesman grin. "Aldo!" I screamed out.

The man pulled his hand away from my chest as I ran over toward Aldo. I absolutely wasn't alright with a guy like Briggs touching me and wasn't exactly sure why he thought it was alright to do it. Aldo didn't seem like the kind of guy who liked to share his women with a chump like Briggs.

"I hate this place, and your friend is a little too handsy for my taste."

Instead of reacting in anger at his friend, Aldo just smiled at me and wrapped his arm around my waist. "It's okay darling, he's just a little bit of an animal," Aldo whispered in my ear.

"No, it's not okay. I'm not some piece of meat that your friends can just touch whenever they want," I said firmly. "Maybe I should just leave."

I felt the tears starting to well up in my eyes and was pretty damn proud of my performance. The problem was, I still felt that damn attraction toward Aldo, and it was a huge driving force in my ability to react the way I was.

There was an animal attraction between Aldo and me that I couldn't deny. Oh, I wanted to deny it. I wanted to leave and go back to Theo and have this all over with, but I couldn't make Aldo mad. It was one last date with him, and I would have everything cleared up and could go back to seeing Theo. "Leave us," Aldo said to Briggs. "We will meet you at dinner in a bit." "Sure," Briggs said as he turned and left quickly.

It was amazing to me how easily Briggs listened to Aldo, yet he had the balls to touch a woman that Aldo had brought with him to the apartment. I wasn't exactly sure what was up with that Briggs guy but was really happy that Aldo had sent him away.

"I'm sorry," I said. "I know I shouldn't have been so mad. But he was just touching me like he didn't care that I was here with you. It was disrespectful."

"But you wouldn't mind if I touched you like that?" Aldo said as he pressed up against me.

My face turned red with desire as his hands grabbed my waist and his eyes looked intently at me again. The power that spilled off of his body was hard to resist. If I hadn't had such deep feelings toward Theo, and if Aldo hadn't been a killer, I might have been willing to sleep with him.

My life was feeling pretty out of control at that moment, and I didn't feel like I was gaining any control any time soon. I tried to continue my acting skills, but the more Aldo looked at me, the less confident I was in my ability to manipulate him.

"I do like the feeling of your hands on my body," I said sweetly as I pressed my hands against his chest.

Our bodies pressed and teased each other, but both of our hands stayed up high around our torsos. I felt his hips as they moved against me and fought the urge to let my hand slide down and into his pants. I wanted to feel his throbbing body in my hands. I wanted to slide my fingers around him and hear him moan as the pleasure built up. But I denied myself that pleasure and Aldo too; instead, I leaned in and tried to kiss him.

Aldo stopped just shy of actually kissing me, and I could tell he was questioning my motives. I wasn't sure myself what my motives were, but I knew that I wanted to feel his lips on mine again. I hated that I wanted him and really didn't want to be so damn attracted to him, but there I was. There he was. And I couldn't help myself.

"Would you like to feel my lips on your body again?" Aldo asked.

I laughed and looked around the apartment. I did my best shy girl look as I glanced at Aldo and then down to the ground. The easy answer was yes, I did want to feel his lips on my body. But I didn't think that was really what he wanted to hear. Theo had said that Aldo liked the tease involved in everything. So I had to try and tease him more and he was going to resist me.

"No one will come in?" I asked. "Does it matter?"

"Yes!" I said as I pressed him away playfully.

But he wasn't about to be denied the pleasure that he wanted. He moved in again and placed his lips on my neck, forcing me to look up into the air as his lips gently kissed me. I involuntarily moaned at the touch of his lips. There was a fine line between acting and reality, and it was clearly hard for me to determine where that line was anymore.

Chapter 12

THEO

The agonizing feeling over making a mistake that you can't fix has got to be as close to torture as a man can get. I felt the vile, disgusting feeling building up in my stomach when I couldn't reach Abby.

Why had I thought that having her go out with Aldo was going to be a good thing? It baffled me that my mind hadn't run through the idea that Aldo was going to totally destroy Abby. Not literally, of course, but he had the ability to make me lose her, and I didn't like that at all. If Aldo wanted her, he would make it happen. He could manipulate and play with her emotions until he got exactly what he wanted.

Of course, I could hope that all he wanted was to play with her a little and tease himself before he sent her back to me. But I knew Abby and found it extremely hard to believe that Aldo would ever be willing to give her up.

The thing that bothered me most was that Abby was going to tease him and play with him all while thinking that she was doing it for me. She wanted to protect me from Aldo's wrath, and I put that thought into her head. It was disgusting how I had manipulated the situation. I should have left her out of it! I should have told her to refuse him if he called, and I would deal with the consequences on my own.

But I had spent the last ten years, at least, avoiding dealing with the reality of my partnership with Aldo. Instead, I relished the extravagant life that I had built and pretended that I had done it on my own hard work; when the truth was I had done it on the hard work of myself but also many others.

My life had all been set up by Aldo, and I did owe him a lot for getting me to where I was. But ten years of my life had to be enough of a payment to him. At what point was I going to be able to move on, and at what point could I sever ties with Aldo without the threat of harm?

It wasn't going to work for me any longer. The mental switch had already

happened, I wanted a real life. I wanted a life I could brag about without lying to people. I wanted to pick my parents up in a private jet
and not have to pretend like it was a friend's jet. I wanted my parents to be proud of what I did for a living instead of me trying to explain that it was from investments and having my father look at me quizzically.

Something inside me was gone. That no holds barred ability to earn money and not give a fuck how I got it. It had just disappeared. Like an ugly guest that was with me for years and suddenly I woke up and they were gone.

When I was young, I remembered thinking that I wanted to be rich so badly. I never had a plan for how I would gain these riches, I just always wanted to have tons of money. Throughout the years of living in New York, I certainly had grown rich, but what had it gotten me? I was still alone and had nothing to really show for my last ten years except for some property and things. I needed to make a change and finally felt like I was ready for something new and different. I was ready to be real with myself and my life.

As I made my way back to my apartment, I shook my head in dismay at the new sobering life I was about to embark on. Certainly, I couldn't keep my apartment if I was getting out of the escort business. I
couldn't keep my jet membership or my cars either. But I didn't really care. I wanted the white picket fence life, and I wanted it with Abby.

"Wow, you look terrible. That's how I feel when I go to the gym too," Kimberly joked as I walked in the door.

She was sitting on the couch with two of her friends, who also worked with VIP Escorts. Megan and Allison had worked with me for several years. They were good girls who treated their men respectfully and almost always got booked a second and even third time. In fact, all three of the women were really good with the men they dated.

"I told Abby she should go out with Aldo again," I said, trying to hide the disgust at my own actions. "Because Aldo threatened me."

I wasn't normally as honest with the women who worked for me. But I didn't have anything to lose anymore.

"Is Abby the girl you like?" Megan asked.

"He loves her; I saw it in his eyes," Kimberly said as she teased me.

It was funny to watch the girls talk about me like I was their best friend, and they had secretly figured out everything about me. I liked feeling that they were concerned about me, at least, and that they actually wanted me to be happy with someone.

"You know what, I might just love her. I haven't actually had love in a long time though, it's hard for me to recognize it."

"Does she make you want to vomit when she is close to you?" Allison asked.

"Eww Allison, that's not love," Kimberly chimed in.

"Seriously ladies, I think I messed this one up. I need some female advice on how I can salvage this."

I didn't actually have many friends. My line of work made it difficult to make guy friends because if they weren't in the business, they wanted to be dating the women I was around. It was impossible to make female friends, they never liked what I did for a living. So pretty much I was relegated to having a slew of beautiful escorts as my friends. I understood that it wasn't the same thing as real friends. But they were going to have to do for the time being.

"So give us a rundown on what is going on." Megan asked as she seriously looked at me and appeared ready to help me with whatever it was I needed.

Megan was a smart girl. She had an MBA from New York University. She wanted to start her own business but had decided to work as an escort to gain the capital she needed. The problem she ran into was the more she worked, the more she wanted to work. The lifestyle and the money were difficult for people to give up. I don't think she had ever really considered giving it up recently, but in the beginning, that was all she talked about. Every time I saw her, she was talking about how much more money she needed to start her business. But a year ago, instead of starting her business, Megan invested all of her money into a lavish new condo. She was back at square one with her business plans but didn't seem to mind it at all.

"Okay, so here's the deal. Jack and I went out to the club to pick up a couple new girls. We thought it was time we got a few more in rotation," I started my story slowly. "This girl Abby that I met, she was sweet and confident, and almost instantly, I knew there was something special between us."

"Your hard on," Allison blurted out.

"Well, she did give me that; of course. But it was different than with other women. I wanted her to like me. Do you know how lame that feels when you're my age and you actually want a woman to like you?"

"Um, that's every day of my life with guys," Kimberly added.

"So I kept thinking that I was going to get over it. The feelings I had toward her were the same other guys would have, and she was going to make a great escort. I took her to Vegas …"

"Oh, the famous Vegas trip, you girls still remember when he took you?" Megan asked as the three women started to talk about their trips.

"Oh, fuck yeah. It was the first truly expensive pair of shoes I've ever gotten," Allison said. "I still have those shoes, they are my lucky fucking shoes."

"Lucky shoes you wanted to fuck or shoes that are just fucking

lucky?" Kimberly teased Allison. "Both."

"Okay, okay, ladies …I know the whole Vegas thing is cliché, I get it. But I really didn't know that I liked her yet. I thought I could still bring her into the business. But actually, let me go back a bit. On the way to the airport, I stopped by to talk with Aldo about what happened with Kimberly and Rocco. He had seen her at a restaurant she worked at, and he liked her. Instantly, I could tell that he wanted to take her out."

"Man, Aldo is one handsome son of a gun," Allison said.

"I know. He's all mysterious and sexy. And damn does he have style. I'd tap that dude all day every day," Megan said in an uncharacteristically enthusiastic manner.

"You go girl," Kimberly added.

"Seriously, what is it about that guy that drives women so bonkers? He's old,

he's like fifty something." "He's still hot as hell. You can't even deny it,"

Megan said.

It was obvious that Megan had a thing for Aldo even long after she had gone on a date with him. I knew he had the ability to charm the ladies, but I thought I was pretty damn good at charming women too, and I never had that kind of reaction from them years down the road. Somehow, Aldo could totally tease a woman, even take her to bed and let his wife watch the whole thing, and everyone was perfectly fine with it. He certainly had some sort of skills that I couldn't even imagine.

"Okay, so anyways. He wanted to take her out, and I said she wasn't going to work for me. It was before I even really knew what I was saying, but I just knew I didn't want him taking her out. Then bam, he offered her ten grands to go to some film industry thing with him, and she took it." "Well, how long had you two known each other at that point?" Megan asked.
"One night."

"Damn right she took his offer. At least you're not in love with a stupid girl!" Kimberly joked.

"Come on ladies, I need real help. Let's fast forward. Yesterday, Aldo is all upset that he thinks I told Abby she was his escort. Of course, I didn't. But it turns out while they were out she kissed him."

"Oh, yeah he hates that," Megan added as she had become our resident expert on all things that pertained to Aldo.

"I know, well he thought she was trying to perform or make him happy, etc. He got pissed off at me and pretty much threatened to kill me. It wasn't the first time he had threatened me, but I thought it would be best to talk to Abby about it. We made up, and I asked her if she would go out with him again and pretend like she didn't know about the escort thing. I asked her to just pretend."

"Wait a minute. Abby knows about the escort business?" Kimberly asked. "She didn't know at all the last time she was here."

"Yeah, Jack told her friend Isabella who then told her."

"And she wasn't pissed off? See, I told you that you had to tell her!"

Kimberly was pretty proud of herself since her advice had been for me to tell Abby all along. So it didn't feel all that great when I had to tell her that

Abby really had been pretty pissed off at me when she found out.

"Oh, yeah, she was pissed off, but we made up," I said with a wink.

"She fucked you even after she found out you had lied to her?" Kimberly said with a shocked expression.

"Yep. I know. We didn't even really fight about it. It was like the fastest argument I've ever had with a woman."

"She likes you," Kimberly added. "The only reason a woman would give up a dream fight like that was if she liked you."

"And he told her to go out with Aldo," Allison said as she started to laugh uncontrollably. "Yeah, what was up with that decision? It doesn't seem very useful at all," Megan added.

"Aldo said he was going to kill me!" I exclaimed in a desperate attempt to get the women to come over to my side.

"Well, he says that to people when he's angry. He loves you like a son; I seriously doubt he would kill you. Did you tell him you liked Abby?"

"Yep, he said I was being childish and living in a fantasy land."

"Yikes," Megan added as she appeared to be thinking through all the scenarios. "Well, the good news is that Aldo doesn't like to sleep with many of his women. He likes to seduce them and get them to fall in love with him. But he only sleeps with a few of them."

"How is that good news?" Allison asked.

"I mean, she might be in love with him when everything is done, but maybe she wouldn't have slept with him."

"Fuck, I need a better plan."

"Well, you're shit out of luck until she reappears from this date she's on with him tonight," Kimberly said, looking to have lost interest in our conversation.

"I'm just supposed to leave it all up in the air and let him have her?"

"What other options do you really have? She's already out with him, right?"

"Yes, but I was hoping you three could come up with some sort of super romantic gesture that would have me stealing her away from him. And not getting murdered," I joked.

"I think you're thinking of Charlie's Angels, that's not us," Allison teased.

"Seriously Theo, you're going to have to wait this one out. If she cares about you, one night with Aldo isn't going to change that. But when you see her next, you need to right these wrongs. You can't let her think you are alright with her going out with Aldo anymore. No more dates with him. Talk to him, it will be fine. I think he's a romantic at heart," Megan said.

I had left out the whole part about me giving up the industry. I didn't want to worry the ladies about their jobs until I had a better idea of what I was going to do with the business. Certainly, I could find someone else to run it. Or like Kimberly said, the women could just do their own thing. But it was harder than they thought to research the guys and make sure they were legitimate. Plenty of men got in contact with me looking for escorts, but I only allowed about half of them to actually take women on dates.

Sometimes the guys just didn't know the real expense that went into an escort. Other times, they were clearly looking for a prostitute and not an escort at all. It was my job to deal with all the losers so I could find decent guys for the women to date. I wasn't sure any of them really understood how much work went into finding decent guys.

"Thanks for your help ladies; I appreciate your point of view. I'll let you know what happens."

The truth was that I really did appreciate their point of view. I didn't have very many true friends, and it was comforting to know that the women who worked for me thought enough of me that they were interested in helping me out. For a brief moment, I felt like I had done right by them throughout the years that they had worked for me.

"We get an invite to the wedding!" Allison said.

"Ha, if Abby and I ever get married, I'll make sure and invite you all."

The women knew me well and didn't seem all that surprised that I had fallen for Abby. I wondered what it was about the way I talked about her that made it seem so realistic for me to want to be with her.

As Kimberly said her goodbyes to Megan and Allison, I made my way into the kitchen to see if I could scrounge something to eat. I couldn't even remember the last time I had eaten; I was so wrapped up in everything that was going on in my life. Plus, I was just plain sick to my stomach with what a jerk I had been over the past few days. If this was what it was like to be love sick; then I could see why people lost so much weight when they fell in love.

"Seriously Theo," Kimberly said as she came into the kitchen after saying goodbye to her friends. "What were you thinking? Why would you let her go out with him?"

The anger in her voice caught me off guard.

"This is bad. You are never going to get out of the business if he gets a hold of her. I didn't want to say this in front of Megan because she's in love with Aldo. But he's a scary mother fucker. My experience with him wasn't good at all."

"What do you mean? You never mentioned this before."

"He was your friend. I couldn't say anything bad about him." "Fuck, what

happened?"

"He's kinky as hell. He wanted me to fuck one of his friends while he watched. Of course, I wanted to make him happy. He was my first real client, and I just wanted to do whatever I was supposed to do. But then he got pissed off when I actually fucked the guy. It was like I couldn't win with him at all."

I was silent because I couldn't think of a damn thing to say. She was right, Aldo never could make up his mind, and certainly the advice I gave Abby might have been the wrong advice for what would work with Aldo. I could only hope that she would continue to deny his requests and not fall into his traps.

"Abby is a smart girl, and whatever happens with Aldo, I'm going to forgive. It is my fault she is in that situation anyways."

"Man, you really don't understand what kind of trouble a girl with Daddy issues can get into with Aldo, do you?"

"What do you mean?"

"Abby's got to be lusting after the guy, and when he starts twisting things around and proposing things to her, she's not going to be able to say no. If he suggests something crazy like turning you into the police, Abby just might do it."

"What the fuck are you talking about?" I said as the conversation went to a place I hadn't even imagined.

"Aldo has a way of getting back at his enemies. If something in your conversation made him believe you are now his enemy, then he is going to use Abby to get back at you. He might do it sexually. He might do it mentally. Or he might set you up with the police. But I wouldn't trust him at all and would be really damn careful of trusting Abby when you're around her. He has a way of getting into a woman's head."

Kimberly appeared to be speaking from experience, but I just couldn't bring myself to talk about it another second longer. There was no way Abby could be turned against me. No way Aldo would do that to me or Abby or that she would be so susceptible to his deceitful ways.

The problem I was having was that I really didn't feel all that confident in anything anymore. Being with Abby and dealing with this whole Aldo situation had really sent me for a loop. I didn't even trust myself or my thoughts any longer.

Chapter 13

ABBY

As Aldo pulled away from me, I felt myself wanting more from him. I wanted his hands on me again, his lips, his hard body. There was more to Aldo than whatever Theo had said, but I couldn't forget the dangers of what Theo had told me either. My mind and body were at odds as I tried to navigate my time with Aldo.

"So, we are going to dinner with your friend?" I asked, trying to change the subject.

"If you won't let me have you right here and right now, then I suppose we should go get some nourishment," he said, smiling at me.

"I need to tell you something, and please don't be angry at me," I said.

It got his attention, and I felt the heat of his green-eyed gaze intensify. He had a small scruff of a grey beard that he fidgeted with, and I could see some of his numerous tattoos very clearly for the first time.

"What is it dear?"

"I fantasized about kissing you after our night together. I liked it a lot."

It did not appear to be what he expected me to say, and he moved quickly toward me and pinned me against the wall of the entryway. I loved the back and forth going on between us. I could see why it aroused Aldo so much and thought it was a bit of a fun game to play.

"Tell me what you thought about," he demanded.

Normally, I wouldn't like it at all when a man demanded something of me. But the way Aldo did it, I felt more like I wanted to. I knew it was a turn on for him; I could see his throbbing member as it pressed against his pants and teased me.

"Oh, no, it's too embarrassing. I shouldn't have said anything," I said as I shyly looked down at the ground. "We can go to dinner now."

"I said to tell me," Aldo said firmly.

His lips were only a few inches from my face, and I could remember what they tasted like still. My body throbbed with its own desires for him, and I wanted to tell him about them. I wanted to excite him, make him happy, so I could urge him to leave Theo alone.

"I was in bed, and when I closed my eyes I pictured us kissing. My body was wet, and I pressed my hips toward you because I wanted to know what your lips would feel like on my wetness."

He was aroused and enthralled with my story. As he pressed his body next to me, I couldn't resist letting my hand slide down and touch his throbbing cock, just briefly before I pulled my hand away.

"I'm sorry, we should go; I don't mean to tease you. It was just a fantasy," I said, knowing he loved his fantasies.

"Tell me more. What else happened in your fantasy?" he asked.

"I felt your tongue on my body; I felt your naked body on top of me. I closed my eyes and imagined you could be mine. I know, it's silly."

"Do you want it to become a reality?" Aldo asked as one of his hands slid between my thighs, and I felt my body react to him.

I didn't answer him, but instead looked around the apartment we were in as if I was waiting for someone to surprise us. Suddenly, I didn't think Aldo was just fantasizing anymore. His voice seemed much more interested in making it a reality.

"Not here," I whispered.

"God, I want to fuck you so badly," he said as his hand pressed higher toward my wetness. "Are you wet thinking about fucking me?"

He didn't wait for an answer, and I soon felt his fingers as they slid inside my panties. Panic ran through me as I decided what to do. Teasing was his thing; I needed to tease him without totally refusing him.

"Oh … God …" I said, closing my eyes and letting his fingers play. "Answer me, do you want to fuck me?" he said again firmly.

"No."

"Your body is telling me something else," Aldo said as he let two of his fingers slide inside of me and pressed his thumb on my clit while he tried to excite me more.

My knees were weak, and I couldn't hide that his fingers felt good. I grabbed onto his neck as I closed my eyes and let him play with me.

"I don't want to fuck you is what I meant," I said breathlessly. "I want you to make love to me." "But your body seems to like what I'm doing right now."

As his fingers moved inside of me, he quickly stroked my clit, and I felt my body building up quickly toward an orgasm. I couldn't stop him and wasn't sure that I wanted to. Then he leaned down and kissed me while his fingers moved inside of me.

I opened my mouth and let his tongue slide in and felt my body releasing as he played with me. "Oh, um … I …" I tried to talk, but I couldn't. "Shouldn't we go to dinner," I asked.

"After you cum."

His lips went back to kissing me and his fingers to making me orgasm, and soon I lost all control and released my inhibitions and came. I could hardly stand and held onto him for support as we continued to kiss. I did like kissing him, I couldn't deny that. But this was a game to Aldo, he didn't have real feelings. I kept reminding myself, this was all a game.

"Now I'm dripping wet, and you want to take me to dinner," I teased him.

Aldo pulled me back into the kitchen and threw me roughly up onto the counter. I had no idea what he was doing until he slid my panties off and put my legs up over his shoulders.

Oh, shit! This was happening.

He gently kissed up my thigh before wrapping his mouth around me and sucking on my juices. His lips were gentle, yet firm, and at first I thought he would just lick me clean, and we would be off to dinner. But I quickly learned that Aldo had much different plans.

I moaned as he used his hands to separate my legs and expose me to him. He looked at my body and then up to me as he smiled. I wasn't sure what my naked exposed body did for him, but it seemed to please him very much.

Quickly, he went back to work licking me, and I felt my body rumbling with excitement. Aldo excited me in a different way than any other man had ever done. It wasn't like I loved him, I knew I didn't have those kinds of feelings for Aldo. But I lusted after him. I wanted him in a way that I couldn't even describe.

My hand moved down to Aldo's hair, and I grabbed it and urged him to continue on. My hips thrust against him, and I felt the pleasure he delivered to me. Without warning, Aldo slid his pinky finger into my ass. It caught me so off guard, I let go of his hair and tried to sit up a little to protest. But it wasn't worth protesting.

Within a minute, I had his pinky in my ass, two fingers inside of me and his thumb rubbing on my clit. All the while Aldo stood over me just watching my body as it reacted to him. I couldn't help moaning and thrusting against him; it all felt so good and overwhelmed me.

I felt so out of control, and I loved it. I knew I shouldn't have liked it so damn much, but I did. Aldo was addicting, being with him made me want to be with him more. I closed my eyes and let go of my inhibitions as he brought my body as close to explosion as he could without actually letting me cum.

"Tell me something," Aldo said in a firm yet calming voice. "Did Theo tell you to go out with me?"

I felt my body panic as I tried to think of the best response. I wasn't thinking of the truth at all, instead, I tried to think of what would help get Theo out of trouble and keep Aldo liking him.

"Today? Or the first date?" I asked as Aldo continued to work on me with his fingers.

It was hard to concentrate with all the pleasure he was giving me, but I closed my eyes and thought of what I should say in response.

"Both."

"On the first day, he didn't really say anything. I asked if he minded that I was going out with you, and he said no. But I didn't tell him I was going out with you today."

It was the truth. I hadn't talked with Theo since Aldo called and said he was coming to pick me up. I wasn't lying at all. Aldo had only given me an hour to get ready before he picked me up at the shelter, I spent the whole time getting ready and didn't call and tell Theo a thing.

"So he doesn't know you're here with me?" Also asked,

seeming delighted at the news. "No."

"Where does he think you are?"

"I don't know. We don't really know each other all that well. I

just met him a few days ago." "Do you like him?"

"That seems like a trick question since you currently have your fingers inside my body," I said with a smile as I looked at Aldo.
"It's not a trick. Do you like him?" "Yes, he's very nice."

"Do you like me?" Aldo asked as he stood over me with my legs on his shoulders and his fingers inside of me.

"I think that is sort of obvious given my current position," I teased.

"So, you like him, but you're here with me. Why is that?" Aldo seemed really suspicious of me, and I felt extremely exposed at the moment.

"I've only known the two of you a couple of days. I don't think that's enough time to make a decision on whether; I'd like to get to know either of you more or not. All I know is I like being here with you right now. Is that alright?"

"Yes."

Aldo, seemed satisfied and quickly started to work his fingers inside of me again. I felt his urging to make me explode and couldn't stop myself as I finally gave in to the delicious feeling of his fingers fucking me.

"Oh, my fucking God," I screamed out as my body twisted and writhed with orgasm.

He liked to watch; I could see that right away as I opened my eyes for a moment and looked at him standing over me. It was turning him on to watch what he did to my body. I had to wonder if he liked watching more than he liked fucking.

I was wrapped up in the moment and shouldn't have said what I did.

"Maybe we should find the bedroom," I said as my body continued to jolt

with orgasm. "You need your nourishment now. Let's go eat," he said

definitively.

He grabbed a towel off the counter and slid it up my thighs as he wiped my cum off of me. Then he gently slid my panties back up my legs and helped me down off the counter. He was quite the gentleman for a guy who just made me cum all over some stranger's counter.

I wrapped my arm around his muscular arm and followed his lead out of the condo and to the elevator.
This time, the sexual tension was much less, and I was exhausted. But I felt safe wrapped up in his arm
and leaning against him. There was just something about Aldo that made me feel undeniably safe. I didn't have uncertainty; I knew damn well that Aldo had the ability to keep me safe no matter what was going on outside the doors of the building.

"Perhaps you should forget about Theo all together, and instead just come be with me," Aldo said nonchalantly as we made it outside.

"Um, how would your wife feel about that?" I teased.

"She would love to have another woman live with us. And I already know that she likes you."

"Are you serious?" I asked in surprise. "You think she would be fine with you just deciding to take me home with you?"

Aldo laughed a bit at what I assumed was my naivety in regards to his home life. I just couldn't imagine that his wife was really okay with all of this. Certainly, after what we had just done, his wife wouldn't be all that excited about having me in his home. I just couldn't fathom a woman being alright with sharing her man like that.

"Instead of dinner with Briggs alone, let's invite my wife to join us,

and you can see for yourself." "What? No. I don't think that's a good

idea at all," I protested.

But the idea seemed to excite Aldo quite a bit, and before I could stop him, he was on the phone to his wife. My eyes must have been twice their size as I looked at him while he talked to her. I just couldn't even imagine what kind of woman was confident enough in her own self to be alright with her husband calling her while he was with another woman.

"Hi darling, I'm with Abigail, and she is so delightful. Would you mind joining us for dinner? We are meeting up with Briggs," Aldo said into the phone. "Oh, yes, I just finished watching her orgasm. You would love her."

"What? No don't tell her that. Oh, my God," I said, covering my eyes. "Do you want to talk to her?" Aldo said as he handed the phone to me.

"No, absolutely no. Oh, God," I said as he put the phone in my hand. "Hello," I said with as much hesitation as I have ever said the word in my entire life.

"Hi Abigail, it's nice to talk to you. Would you mind if I came to dinner with you all. I don't want to spoil your evening."

"Um, it's fine."

"Great, I'll see you in a bit. I can't wait to talk with you more," Aldo's wife said before she hung up.

"Um, she's coming to dinner," I said with my eyes wide as I looked at Aldo. "I feel like I'm going to pass out."

We were on the street corner, and I really did feel like I could pass out. It was impossible to imagine how chipper and nice she was. I didn't know what was going on, but I certainly wasn't prepared to deal with it. My life felt like it was spinning all over the place, and I couldn't get control over it at all.

"You're okay, let's grab some water and sit down. Or do you think you can make it to the restaurant?"

Aldo had his arm around my back and was supporting me as I held onto him. My legs were weak from a combination of the events that had gone on in the apartment and the sheer shock of what I had just heard on the phone.

"This is wild," I said under my breath.

"You know what? I think I've got another wild idea that might just make you pass out," Aldo said as he sat me down on a bench nearby.

"What?" I asked, almost afraid to hear what he had to say.

"It's a surprise darling," Aldo said, taking just enough steps away from me so I couldn't hear who he was calling.

I wasn't cut out for this kind of stuff. Sure, I didn't mind a little fun every now and then, but I couldn't keep up with Aldo's lifestyle, that was for sure. He was exhausting. I didn't know how he managed all his businesses, his women and still had energy to pick up new women. I decided that he must do drugs or something to keep his energy up at that high a level. Or maybe he was one of those super fit vitamin freaks. He did have muscles for days. Perhaps he took a lot of those natural energy supplements that made it possible for him to never need sleep.

My eyes were fixated on Aldo's lips as I tried to figure out who he was talking to. But there was no use, so I finally just gave up and pulled my own phone out of my purse to see what I had missed.

Of course, I had missed calls from both Isabella and Theo. There was also a voice message from Theo, which I couldn't wait to hear so I dialed in and listened to it right away.

"Abby, you don't need to go out with Aldo. I'm sorry, it was stupid for me to ask that of you. He's dangerous, you shouldn't be around him. If you get this before your date, call me. If you get this after your date, still call me. I'm sorry for being such a weird jerk."

I laughed at his message. I didn't think he was a weird jerk at all. I also didn't mind being out with Aldo. Despite still not knowing if he was going to pay me or not, I liked being around him. That probably said a lot about the weird sort of jerk that I was.

"Recovered? Ready to eat?" Aldo asked as he grabbed me by the hands and

pulled me up. "Starving."

"Great, this is going to be one fantastic dinner." Aldo had a mischievous look in his eyes that I really didn't know what to do with. Dinner was certainly going to be one crazy night. "How much did you say you needed to help your sisters out?" Aldo asked.

It was weird that he was bringing up my family at such a moment, but I was inclined to be honest with him.

"It's a lot of money. I think it's too much. I'm just going to have to move them into an apartment or something."

"How much?"

"It's four hundred thousand dollars for everything. The back mortgage, taxes, and our family's business. But they are going to sell the business off as soon as they can get hold of it so they will be able to pay a lot of it back."

"Deal."

"What? Wait, what do you mean?" I asked.

"You go along with my plans for dinner, and I'll give you the four hundred

thousand that you need." "What? No. That's too much; I can't take that from you. I don't accept handouts."

"I thought you might say that. So I'm making it a job. You need to convince everyone at our dinner table that you want to be with me. No matter who shows up. Even if it's the president of the United States. You convince them that you want to be with me."
"But your wife is coming to dinner." "I know. Convince her."

"And that Briggs guy." "Yes, convince him."

"Who else is coming?" I asked.

"It's a surprise, it is a man. But you will have to convince him as well. One simple dinner and all your family's troubles will be over. Well then of course I'll also want you to come home with my wife and I and live with us."

"Live with you?"

"Yes, I think my wife will agree that you will make a great addition." "What

about Theo?" I asked.

"If you tell him I've made you this offer, I will make sure he is turned into the police and he spends years and years behind bars. Theo wouldn't bat his eye at this kind of money. Don't put a man you hardly know ahead of your own family's stability."

"Can I think about it?"

"What is there to think about? It is your sisters, your blood. Don't you want to protect them?"

Chapter 14

THEO

"Dinner? Like right now?" I asked when Aldo said he wanted me to come and meet him.

It was odd. Aldo seemed to be pretty pissed off at me, and I didn't think he wanted to have a meal with me anytime soon. Certainly, there had to be something else going on. I thought that Abby was still with him, but he didn't say on the phone. He simply told me to come have dinner with him. So of course, I obliged and got my ass ready and headed down to the restaurant.

Perhaps something had happened between him and Abby and she had convinced him to let me and her be together. Or maybe it was something else entirely; I just couldn't decide what to make of it all.

I wanted to get things settled between Aldo and me, and I wanted him to be done with Abby. I couldn't stand the idea of her going out with him any longer and was happy to meet with him over dinner and discuss things.

Over the years, Aldo and I had gotten to know each other very well, and he had never threatened to kill me before. Although I knew he was obviously a very dangerous person, he and I had always been on the same side, and I wanted to make things right with him again.

There were so many years of history between the two of us that I just couldn't imagine things going so horribly wrong all over one girl. Aldo could have his pick of any woman that he wanted and apparently his wife was even alright with that sort of thing; there was no reason for him to pick Abby. She didn't love him and didn't want to be with him, I knew that. Over dinner, I would simply explain the situation to him and ask him nicely to stop going out with her and let me date her myself. Surely our ten years of friendship was enough that he would be willing to do that for me.

I grabbed my things and made it to the small restaurant that Aldo had suggested. I had been to Rubio's once before, and it struck me as a weird place. They had food from America, Italy, and France; it was like they couldn't decide who they really wanted to be.

When I walked into the restaurant, I was looking for Aldo, but I couldn't find him at all. I looked around the front of the restaurant and even glanced into the back, but he was nowhere to be found. For a brief moment, I thought it had been some sort of trick to get me out of the house, but then I decided I was being a little paranoid.

"Is Aldo Gioacchino here?" I asked like the woman at the front would know exactly who I was talking about.

Fortunately for me, she did know who I was talking about and quickly took me through to a private room where he was. But Aldo wasn't there alone. He had Abby and his wife with him at the table. I was more confused than ever. The three of them looked pretty damn comfortable together, and I got a sick feeling in my stomach.

There had only been a few other times in my life where I truly felt like things were going wrong and my gut had warned me. But at that moment, I felt it and I wanted to turn and leave right away. The only thing that kept me there in that room was the fact that Abby was there with them, and I didn't want to leave her there. I had no idea why Aldo wanted to have dinner with me and Abby and his wife, but I was going to stick around; no matter what my gut was telling me to do.

"Theo, it's so nice of you to join us," Aldo said in an unusually pleasant tone.

Considering the last time we had talked I pretty much got threatened with murder, I didn't really see how he was so chipper all of a sudden now that I was there to have dinner with them.

"Abby, would you like to have Theo sit by you?" Aldo asked.

Abby looked at me with wide eyes and then back to Aldo as she obviously was trying to figure out what she should say. She looked lost as she sat there, and I wanted to just grab her and pull her out of the restaurant. Nothing about the situation seemed good, and I felt like something bad was about to happen. I felt the feeling so strongly in my gut that I could hardly think about anything else except getting Abby and leaving that restaurant as fast as possible.

"Sure," she finally answered.

So I took a seat to the right of Abby and Aldo, and his wife sat on the other side of them. There was an empty chair on my right, and I assumed that it was for Briggs when he decided to arrive. But Briggs was notoriously late for things, so I didn't expect he would be coming anytime soon.

"Theo, it's so nice to see you again," Nicole, Aldo's wife said as I sat down.

"You too Nicole. How's the lawyer world treating you?"

"It's very busy, but I love it. Thank you for asking."

Nicole was pretty uptight, and it was weird to me that things worked out between her and Aldo. But I figured every couple had their own weird things, and whatever happened in their private life seemed to work for them just fine.

Nicole was a beautiful woman, and she reminded me of Abby in a lot of ways. Not because of their looks, Nicole and Abby didn't look alike, but in the way they carried themselves and interacted with the world. Nicole seemed to be able to adapt herself to whatever situation she was in, and she could easily change from being very cold and unfriendly to being personable and warm. It was a special gift that I was sure had helped her in dealing with Aldo over the years.

"Hi Theo," Abby said shyly.

"How are you?" I asked quietly, although I could tell that Aldo could hear me.

"I'm good. Starving to death here, though. Hopefully they will bring some food."

Abby had barely spoken the words before Aldo raised his hand at the waiter and did this weird number thing with his fingers. Within five minutes, our table was covered with a wide variety of different foods.

I hated that Aldo felt like Abby was his and he was going to impress her by having food delivered to the table quickly just because she said she was hungry. In fact, I hated everything about sitting at that table with Aldo and Abby so close together. My body continued to scream at me to grab Abby and leave, but I fought myself and tried to sit and figure out what exactly was going on and why Aldo had brought me there.

I had a little pull with the some of the restaurants I went to, but nothing quite like Aldo had. He had been around much longer than I, and he was able to really get people to do almost anything that he wanted them to do. Sometimes, I thought they were afraid of him and other times I just thought that they really wanted to please him. But for whatever reason, they always clamored to make Aldo happy.

"So Nicole, this is Abigail, isn't she delightful," Aldo said as he started to talk to his wife. "I think you two will get along great."

"Yes sweetheart, she is," Nicole said, a little bewildered at why her husband was making such a bold statement. "Abigail darling, why don't you switch spots with Aldo so us girls can talk, and we can leave those men to their boring conversations."

Aldo jumped up out of his seat and pulled Abby's chair out so she could move over to sit by Nicole. It was the last thing that I wanted to happen. But I would rather have Abby talking to Nicole than talking to Aldo, so it was good enough for me. It seemed incredibly odd to me how Aldo and Nicole were acting, though, and I didn't like it one bit.

"I have a proposition for you, Theo," Aldo said as he sat down and turned toward me.

The women were both talking to each other, so it didn't look like they could hear us, or they weren't paying attention at least. This was it, this was the reason he had brought me to the restaurant with Abby and his wife. I was eager to hear what the proposition was that Aldo had for me.

I could still remember the very first dinner the two of us had when Aldo had made the proposition to me to fund my business with him. He offered to loan me the necessary money to take over his escort business and make it my own. Over the years, he had stopped putting money into the business and hadn't been hiring new girls at all. He had just started to transition himself into more legal avenues and was wanting someone else to run his smaller operations.

Even though I was young, I knew enough that I didn't want to be controlled by Aldo, so I offered to pay him a stipend each month if the business could be mine alone without his control. It was a bold move for me to make a counter offer to a man like Aldo, but it all worked out in the end, and I gained sole control of a brand new escort business and Aldo loaned me the money I needed to get it back on its feet.

"Sure, what is it?"

"You want out, right?" Aldo asked.

I wasn't sure if it was a trick question or not. But I decided to just go with it. Aldo had a way of asking a question that seemed totally normal but was really a trick. I thought about it for a moment and then decided there couldn't be a trick to this question and I should just answer it.

"Yes."

"Okay, here's the deal. You give up Abigail to me, and I'll let you shut down your escort business and live the legal life if that you want."

He knew damn well that the only reason I wanted to get out of the escort business was because of Abby. What good would it do to get out of the business if I didn't have her? It was a trick question and a rotten one at that. Aldo always wanted his own way; he never really cared what was best for anyone else, and I knew he didn't care what Abby really wanted.

"Aldo, I want Abby," I said decisively.

"I thought you might say that. So I have another proposition for you. Share her. You go off and have your happily ever after, but you let her come play with me when I want her."

"No," I said without thinking at all.

There was absolutely no possible way I was going to share Abby with Aldo. I had finally come to the conclusion that she was the one for me, and I wasn't going to give that up just because Aldo wanted to have her too. No, there was absolutely no way I was going to let Aldo have Abby.

Well, unless that was what Abby wanted. I guessed that I didn't really know Abby's feelings on the matter, but I couldn't imagine that she would want to be shared between Aldo and myself. I just didn't think that was something Abby was into.

"Don't you want to talk it over with her? Maybe she would be alright with the offer?" Aldo said as he turned to look at his wife and Abby talking.

Nicole had her hand stroking Abby's hair, and I literally almost freaked out on them all. Aldo and his freak of a wife were trying to set up some weird foursome or something like that, and I didn't want any part of it. No I wasn't going to share Abby with him or his wife, and I didn't need to talk to her about it.

"Aldo, Abigail and I are getting along famously. Thank you so much for inviting me to dinner with you all," Nicole said in a weird Stepford wife sort of voice.

"Abby, can I talk to you for a minute?" I said as I stood up, walked over and grabbed her.

I felt like a brute grabbing his woman and pulling her away from other people. But I couldn't just stand by and watch as she got sucked into their weird web. Abby was an innocent Kansas girl, she certainly didn't have any idea what she was getting herself into.

I expected that Aldo was going to object to me talking with Abby alone, but he didn't seem to have a problem at all. Instead, Aldo just smiled and winked at Abby as I pulled her away. Something was going on, and I didn't like it at all. I really want to just grab Abby and leave. Certainly it was a bluff that Aldo was going to kill me, that was a bit dramatic. He wanted me alive so I could keep giving him money, and he could keep in control.

"Let's just get out of here. You and me, whatever happens I don't care," I said as I held onto her.

I really didn't even care what had happened between Abby and Aldo up to that point. It had been my fault for forcing her to go out with him again. I desperately wanted to leave with Abby and would have picked her up and thrown her over my shoulder if it had been an acceptable thing to do.

"Theo, Aldo is a nice guy; I'm not going to just take off on him," Abby said with a sweet smile. "I think I'd like to spend more time with him."

Her voice was very monotone, and I knew something was going on. The Abby that I knew wouldn't have talked like that, and she certainly wouldn't have wanted to spend time with Aldo over me. I couldn't help thinking she was doing this just to keep Aldo from getting angry, and I needed her to know that it didn't matter anymore.

Couldn't she see what was going on? Did she have some sense that Aldo was just playing her and didn't really care about her at all? She wasn't as street smart as her friend Isabella, but I knew Abby was smart and knew she could see through Aldo.

Even if she couldn't see through him, I had told her about him. I had told her that he had murdered people before. How could that be okay for her? I didn't know what was going on, but I wanted to shake Abby out of it.

"Abby, what the hell is going on? I know it's my fault for telling you that he was dangerous and you should go out with him again. Don't hold that against me, please. You need to get away from him."

"Theo, you're being a little melodramatic," she said to me again in a flat monotone voice. "I want to be here with Aldo."

"Melodramatic? What are you talking about? His freak wife is petting you like you're her dog and what
… they are going to take you back to their place and keep you as their pet or something?"

Abby laughed at me, but she turned around and wouldn't look at me. That was when I knew for sure that something was going on. Abby had always made eye contact with me ever since the very first night we had met. The connection we had when our eyes locked onto each other was far and above something that just couldn't compare to anything else. She didn't want to be saying the things she was; I felt it, and when she wouldn't look at me, I knew it for sure.

"Theo, I'm fine. You know we have only known each other for a few days. I think it's probably time for us to take a break from whatever this is that is going on."

"Look at me Abby; I don't know what you're talking about, but you need to look at me when you say this shit."

I grabbed onto her and twisted her around so I could see her. There were tears in her eyes. I didn't know why, but it couldn't be good.

"Go on Theo, I'm staying with them for dinner," she said as she walked back

to the table. "Then so am I," I said defiantly.

"You two done with your little talk?" Aldo asked.

"Yes, Theo was just telling me that I had forgotten some things at his place. I told him I would get them another time."

"Aldo, is Abigail going to be joining us tonight?" Nicole asked. "Only if I'm joining you as well," I chimed in.

Aldo, looked at me with a look so filled with distain that I thought he might actually punch me right there. I didn't know exactly what his end game was with Abby, but I wasn't about to make the same mistake I had made earlier. I wasn't leaving her with him.

"Well, that's a delightful little surprise for me now isn't it?" Nicole said as she eyed me.

Instantly, I tensed up at the idea of sleeping with Aldo's wife. Was that what they were into? She was a very attractive woman, but she wasn't really my type. Nicole Gioacchino was very uptight and proper. Well, at least on the outside she was. Who the hell knew what she was like behind closed doors.

I thought Aldo might chime in with something interesting to add, but he just sat down next to me with a look of amusement on his face. He had under-estimated me, and I wasn't about to let him have his way. But there was one thing I needed to prepare for: retribution. If things turned out badly this evening, then certainly I wasn't going to end up getting out of anything alive.

"Do we need anything else?" the waitress said as she stopped by the table. "I need vodka," Abby said a little too loudly.

Aldo pressed his hand on her back and leaned in to whisper something to her. Whatever he said made her laugh, and I was instantly jealous. Why was he making her laugh? Why the hell was she actually laughing?

"So Aldo, you want to keep my girlfriend for yourself do you?" I said boldly.

It wasn't politically correct to say such a thing directly to Aldo, and I certainly knew that Abby didn't like being called my girlfriend. But I wasn't about to sit back and let any man walk all over me like Aldo was trying to do. He needed to understand that I wasn't just going to be alright with whatever his plan was.

He laughed at me and again leaned in and whispered in Abby's ear. I couldn't take it another moment.

"Doesn't it bother you that your husband is sitting there flirting with my girlfriend?" I asked Nicole, although by this point I was pretty sure she was crazy herself.

"Jealousy isn't something that I enjoy much at all. I prefer to skip that emotion in my life. As for Abigail, I think she is delightful, and I've fantasized about tasting her since the moment I saw her in the restaurant. It was Aldo that denied me the opportunity of getting her number at that time. So I'm eternally grateful to you for bringing her into our life again."

"This is craziness, Abby. Just come with me. I don't know what's going on here, but we need to just go back to my place and talk."

"Like I told you already, Theo; I'm going to stay and have dinner with Aldo and his wife," Abby said without even looking at me.

"Theo, you are welcome to stay with us, and I think Nicole would love to have you return to the house with us as well. But I think maybe you should have a drink to cool down a little."

"Cool down … you want me to cool down? Just hours earlier you were threatening to kill me because I didn't want to tell Abby about the escort business and now here you are dragging her into your sick twisted marriage. You know what Aldo, you can kiss my ass. I'm not fucking your wife for you, and I'm certainly not going to sit back and watch you fuck my girl!" I screamed, standing up and hurrying over toward Abby.

I reached for her to pull her away, but this time Aldo did stop me. His arm grabbed hold of mine, and I felt the power in his grip.

"Leave without her," Aldo said.

"Abby, please come with me. I know it's crazy. I know you probably hate me and this is all because of that, but please just come with me. I'll make it up to you."

"Theo, this is your last chance to leave," Aldo said, standing up and facing me.

Then, without thinking at all, I cocked my fist back and let it land smack dab on Aldo's jaw. For a man of his age, he took a punch really well because he barely moved at all when I hit him.

"Theo, no!" Abby exclaimed. "You have to leave; he's going to kill you."

There! That was it! Aldo had threatened to kill me if Abby didn't stay with him. That mother fucker had her going along with his plan because he was threatening me. I felt the anger building inside of me and was ready to punch him again.

"Leave now or she's going to get hurt," Nicole said as she held a black 9mm gun toward me and then slid it toward Abby's head.

The whole situation had just turned insane in that moment. Abby looked at me in fear, but it seemed like she was more in fear of my life than her own.

"Tell him he can leave now," Aldo said to Abby.

"Theo, this has all gotten out of control. I don't love you; I barely even like you. Please leave me alone," Abby said, but this time she looked me right in the eyes, and I knew she didn't mean a single word of it.

Reluctantly, I backed away from the table to leave.

"I guess life isn't about the lemons, it's about the lemonade you make," I said, looking Abby right in the eyes.

I saw a small grin flash across her face, and Nicole put her gun back in her purse; then I turned and left the restaurant. I wasn't giving up, but I knew when I needed to back away.

Chapter 15

ABBY

I thought Theo was going to get himself shot. He was so angry, so out of control, I honestly didn't think he was going to leave like he did. I couldn't believe the mess of a situation I had gotten myself into.
Surely, I had a way out, but for the life of me, I couldn't figure out what it was. "I'm glad he's gone, now we can finish our meal in peace," Aldo said.

I certainly didn't feel like eating anything. And I couldn't figure out how they expected me to just sit there like nothing had happened. Nicole had literally just pointed a gun to my head and threatened me, now I was supposed to simply sit next to them and eat my meal like nothing had happened.

"Where is Briggs? I thought he was supposed to be here a half of an hour ago," Nicole asked.

I just sat there in silence as the two of them talked, not having a thing to say to either one of them. I should have known right away when Aldo made me such an offer that he was going to have Theo there as the person I needed to convince. It was very clear to me that Aldo was some sort of sick man and his wife was too. Every desire I had once had for him was gone and had been replaced by hatred.

No longer did it matter to me if I had money at all. I would just send for my sisters to come stay with me. If the three of us were all working, we could certainly afford some sort of apartment. Or maybe even we could stay with Theo although I suspected he wasn't going to want to have anything to do with me after what had just happened.

"Let's just eat darlings; I know for a fact that Abigail is hungry," Aldo said as he touched my hand.

It took every piece of willpower that I had not to yank my hand away from him in disgust. But I couldn't show my true feelings. Not after what I just saw, not after knowing that Nicole had a gun, and she was willing to shoot people.

I was starving, so I decided to make good use of my time and eat the food that was out. I had gotten myself into quite the mess and wasn't going to get out of it right away. Certainly, there was a way to figure this mess out; I just wasn't seeing it just yet.

"Hey guys, what did I miss?" Briggs said as he came galloping up to the table out of breath.

"Well, Nicole almost shot Theo in the head," Aldo said nonchalantly as he

took a bite of chicken. "Oh, man, nice! Wish I could have been here for that.

Did he run away crying?"

"Not crying, but I think he got the point."

"That guy, man you have given him his entire life. The nerve of him to piss you off enough that your wife wanted to shoot him."

Briggs had no idea why Nicole had put a gun to Theo's head, and he didn't care at all either. It was clear that Briggs just sucked up to Aldo to get what he wanted. Probably some free sex with escorts and real estate deals. Briggs was even more disgusting than guys like Aldo because he was willing to do anything just to please the man.

The whole evening had changed for me when Aldo pulled me toward him and whispered in my ear that he was going to shoot Theo in the head if I didn't laugh like something was funny. It took me a minute to understand he was serious, but then he squeezed my arm so hard I felt like he was going to break it. So of course, I did as he said.

How could I have been so wrong about him? I thought as I sat and watched Aldo, his wife and Briggs eat dinner and act as if nothing at all had happened. Clearly, I wasn't as good a judge of character as I had thought I was. I should have listened to Theo. Really, I should have listened to my own damn heart.

This was my life on an even larger scale. I found peace, or happiness, and then I searched to destroy it. Theo and I had something. We had something that was different than I had with any other guy in the past, and I went and destroyed it in search of money. It was ridiculous. Theo even offered to give me whatever money I needed, but I still went off in search of the money from Aldo. My stubborn pride made me feel like I had to earn it, and I knew damn well how Aldo was going to have me earn it. Sure, I tried to think he really just wanted to spend time with me, but I knew better.

Why did I do this crap to myself? Surely, I was worth having happiness. But every time the opportunity for happiness presented itself in my life, I ran away. Or worse yet, when happiness was right there, I stomped on it and then ran away. I was a horrible person, and Theo would be better off without me in the long run.

Theo was a good guy, sure he owned an escort business, and if any normal girl was bringing him home to their mother that wouldn't look good. But I didn't have a mother to bring him home to and had pretty much been living the escort life the last few years in New York City. My fees were much cheaper than the women that worked for Theo. I simply required a meal, some drinks and a bed to sleep in; all in exchange for my company.

It was funny to me that I had judged Theo for the decisions he made to become successful when he came to New York, yet I had made some pretty horrible decisions myself.

"Briggs, tell Abby about your sexual fetishes. I think she would be enlightened to know my fetishes are not as weird as she might think," Aldo demanded as he drank his wine.

"It's alright, I'm sure they are plenty weird," I said in as casual a tone as I could muster.

There was no way I wanted to hear about what Briggs liked to do in the bedroom. Briggs was a slightly balding older man with a bulging belly and slicked back hair. If there was a stereotype for what a used car salesman looked like, it would have fit Briggs exactly.

"I insist," Aldo added.

"Sure thing Aldo," Briggs said as he slapped his food in his mouth and began talking while he chewed. "I like to hear screaming. Any kind of screaming. I like when I ram myself into her ass and she screams.
When I slap her around and she screams? Pretty much the scream of a woman turns me on so much I need to fuck her brains out until she stops screaming."

I just sat there and stared at Briggs as I tried to hide the disgust on my face. I could only assume that it
was some sort of warning that if I didn't behave myself, they were going to make me go with Briggs. So, I did my best to act the part that had gotten me invited to the dinner in the first place.

"Nicole, I don't know about you, but I prefer a much gentler approach," I said as I let my hand slide over to her leg.

"Yes, these men can be such Neanderthals sometimes," she said as her face lit up.

I could see in her eyes that she liked me flirting with her, and since she was the one with the gun, I figured it was probably a pretty damn good time for me to start flirting with her. I needed to do absolutely anything I could to make it out of that damn dinner alive.

"I can still remember the moment I met you," I said, looking at Nicole. "I remember thinking your life was so perfect, that you were so perfect."

My gaze didn't look away from Nicole as I tried to convince her that I believed she was as perfect as she clearly believed she was.

"You are so kind. I knew it when I saw you in that restaurant too. You looked at me and talked to me instead of to Aldo. Most of the young waitresses gravitate toward him, but you were respectful and sweet and just so perfect."

"I wouldn't have gone out with a married man, ever. Please know that I didn't know he was married when I accepted his first invite," I said with enthusiasm, even though it was clear that Nicole and Aldo didn't really have the married and unattainable thing going for them.

"Oh, I know. I told him he would have to keep things platonic with you until he explained our situation."

"Are you two ladies going to fuck because I would like to watch that," Briggs said as he continued to slop his food around in his mouth.

"We are, it's going to be romantic and hot and so amazing, but you're not invited," Nicole said.

Aldo laughed at the interaction but didn't chime in. It was clear that although he was definitely in charge of all his business-related matters, it was Nicole that was in charge of their sexual freakiness. I wondered if Aldo had always been into threesomes and group encounters or if it was his relationship with Nicole that had perpetuated it.

So my goal was no longer to concentrate on making Aldo happy; instead, I needed to make Nicole happy. If Nicole liked me and wanted to be with me, then I would be in the good graces of Aldo for sure.

"Aldo, how did you get so lucky to find such a beautiful and kind woman to marry you?" I asked in a light-hearted tone.

"Me, oh no, it's Nicole that got lucky," he joked.

We continued on with our meal and the absurd conversations that came with it. My mind was beyond baffled by the ease at which Aldo and Nicole could switch from wanting to kill someone to having a flirting romance with them. But I played along the best I could as we finally finished our meal and got ready to leave the restaurant.

My idea was that I could make an excuse that I couldn't go home with them. Certainly, they didn't expect me to give up everything and go live with them right away. But I had learned there was no real telling what Aldo and his wife were thinking, so I was prepared for almost anything.

"Let's get you ladies home," Aldo said as he pulled my chair out and then Nicole's. "It was nice seeing you Briggs, I'll let you know about the apartment, but I'm not really feeling it right now."

"Yeah, I've got some other ideas for you if you'd like. Just give me a call when you're ready." "Sure," Aldo said as he shook hands with Briggs and then turned his attention back toward me. "You did very well tonight. I think you deserve what I promised you."

I really didn't care about his stupid money any longer and wasn't going to take it. There was no way in hell I would ever get away from him if I took that money. I knew that for a fact. But I couldn't just deny him; I had to figure out a different way.

"Thank you, but there's no big hurry. I like spending time with you, and I'm curious about your wife." "You've never been with a woman?" Nicole asked with eagerness in her eyes.

"No, I haven't."

"Oh, Aldo how could she be any more perfect?"

"I'm not sure she could be," Aldo said as he grabbed me and pulled me toward him.

It was uncomfortable to have Aldo showing me attention when his wife was right there, but I decided to go with it and pretend that it didn't bother me.

His lips pressed against mine, and it was the final confirmation that whatever lust I had once had toward him was gone. At that moment, all I could think about was how badly I wanted to be with Theo. How the simplicity of a real relationship seemed like heaven compared to whatever the hell was going on with Aldo and his wife at the moment.

I pressed my lips against Aldo's and tried to hide my utter disgust with him. No longer did he look cool and hip. Instead, he had started to look like a desperate fifty something-year-old man who was doing whatever was necessary to hold onto his youth and his relationship with his wife. I couldn't be part of such a weird relationship.

"Let's get you home so I can play with you," Nicole said as she grabbed my hand and pulled me away from Aldo while we were still kissing.

Although Nicole had been the one who held a gun to Theo and then toward me, I felt much less threatened by her than I did by Aldo. Perhaps the reason she carried a gun was because of Aldo. Or perhaps I should have been more afraid of her than him. But I didn't get the vibe that she had ever murdered someone or even actually shot her gun. But from Aldo, I certainly felt like he had experience taking the life of people who crossed him.

"I'm exhausted," I said as I wrapped my arm around Nicole's and walked with her. "And I'm not sure that chicken is sitting all that well in my stomach."

"You know, I was thinking the same thing. They really should have the health department check them out and make sure they are cooking their food thoroughly enough. I would hate for anyone to get sick from their chicken," Nicole added.

It was like I was back in the olden days when I first arrived in New York. I had placed a small tidbit of information at Nicole's foot, and she had run with it. I felt like it was a special talent that I had and hoped it would allow me to get out of the evening's festivities that I was sure Nicole and Aldo were planning.

"So please don't be mad at me for asking this, but what is the sleeping arrangement. I don't want to be rude or do anything that is inappropriate."

"You are just the sweetest thing," Nicole said as she opened the car door and we both climbed in. "I'm sure we will figure it out as the night goes. Nothing to worry about. I promise I won't be offended by anything you do."

I seriously doubted she wouldn't be offended by anything I did. I had the great ability of offending people, even when I didn't think I was offending them. Sometimes, I just clearly didn't understand what was going on, but other times I was just speaking from my heart and not thinking things through. But the fact that I was going home with Aldo and his wife who both wanted to ravage me in their own ways, I knew for a fact I was going to offend someone before the night was over. It was my only way out of the whole deal.

"Okay, just promise you will let me know if there is something I'm doing wrong. I really don't want to offend anyone," I said in a childlike quiet voice. "Could you tell me where the restroom is? I'm not
feeling well," I said when we walked into their house.

As I rushed into the bathroom and locked the door, I quickly pulled my phone out and sent a text to Theo. "I'm at Aldo's house. I'm trying to get free. Please forgive me."

I didn't know if Theo was going to understand at all what I had done or why I had done it, but I had to hope that he would. There was no way I was staying with Aldo and Nicole, and certainly I couldn't go back to the way things were before Theo had come into my life.

I grabbed a cup from the counter and filled it with water as I went to the toilet and started to make heaving sounds.

"Oh, man, this chicken sure isn't sitting well," I said loudly. "Are you alright?" Nicole asked.

I splashed the water on my face and then made a horrible vomiting noise as I dumped the cup of water into the toilet.

"Oh, God, nope … that does not look as good going out as it did go in," I said.

As I flushed the toilet, I looked in the mirror to make sure my face looked sweaty and my makeup had smeared a little. I was surprisingly good at faking being ill. It had been what had saved me from sleeping with dozens of men over the years. Certainly, it could save me from one woman and her plans for me that evening.

Chapter 16

THEO

"I need to speak to someone in charge," I said to the police officer behind the counter.

She didn't look at me with the same urgency that I was looking at her, though. It was like she didn't even care that I was there, standing in her police precinct, trying to turn in one of the most famous men in New York.

I was desperate to get someone to help me and felt so out of control at that moment. My body was buzzing with a need to save Abby, and I literally would have done anything I could to get her away from Aldo. For the first time in my life, I really knew what love was. As I stood in front of the police officer, I was totally willing to give up my fortune and my freedom if it meant that Abby would be safe.

"I am a police officer; you can speak to me," she said, barely looking up from the paperwork she had in front of her.

"I have evidence against Aldo Gioacchino, and I'd like to talk to someone in charge."

The mention of Aldo's name was finally enough to get the woman's attention, and she looked up at me.
She eyed me over, and whatever she was looking for seemed to be there as she nodded her head in
affirmation and went to grab someone. I didn't really care who it was I talked to, but I needed to turn Aldo in. If that meant turning myself in, then so be it, but I couldn't let him control Abby and threaten me.

Over the years, I had been present for many of the atrocious acts that Aldo had committed. I had watched him tell his guys to strangle a man. I had watched him in action when the Mayor's daughter overdosed at his house and they had to bring her to the ER. I knew more about Aldo than he knew about me, so he should have been more afraid of me than he was.

"What's your name kid?" A very official looking man in uniform said as he came to the desk. "Theodore Stern," I replied.

"Mr. Stern, you look like an upstanding citizen, and I can appreciate you want to follow the law and all, but are you sure you want to turn in information on Aldo Gioacchino?" The officer asked.

He didn't look excited at all that I wanted to turn Aldo in; in fact, he seemed to be trying to talk me out of it. In my mind, I had thought that the police would be clamoring to get hold of a bigwig like Aldo. I had expected that they would have been following him for years and trying to find just the right time to arrest him.

But deep down, I knew that he had worked really hard to pay off a lot of the police force and that was how he had avoided jail for so many years. That was always why I had avoided investigations and jail over the years. But I still genuinely thought if they had an inside guy like myself, the police would have wanted to get Aldo and put him behind bars.

I understood Aldo wasn't the kind of guy you wanted to mess around with unless you could actually catch him. The police weren't going to go after him for some little thing that he was going to get off from. And they certainly weren't going to go after him for something that they couldn't prove. But I knew so much about Aldo, how could I not be helpful?

"I know him well sir, and I understand your concerns. He's also got my girlfriend held up at his house right now, and I'm inclined to tell you everything I know about him over the last decade of working directly with him."

"Let's get a room," the officer said.

I followed him to a small conference room and was prepared to put my entire statement on video or audio or something. I was even prepared to write it down if it took me all day. Whatever they needed to lock him up, I was ready.

"Is this room videotaped? You are probably going to want that in case something happens to me after I tell you all of this," I said, thinking of the possibility that Aldo would actually kill me after finding out what I had done.

"Kid, there is no video or audio in this room. It's just you and me. Tell me what's going on." "Officer Reynolds," I said as I looked at his nametag. "I think we need a video tape."

"See right there, that's how I know what you're about to tell me is the truth. Only a man who really knew Mr. Gioacchino would understand the dangers of giving this information to the police. How about let's start with why he had your girl."

I tried to explain everything to him. I didn't hold back. It was what I needed to do to get Abby out of his hands. The officer was kind to me; he didn't make a big thing about me running an escort business or having feelings for a woman I had only known for a few days. He shook his head and listened to my story with empathy. I thought perhaps he needed to hear what it was I had to say before he brought me to a questioning room to get it all on tape.

"Mr. Stern, I sympathize with what's going on with your girl. But I don't think the New York police department is in a position to take on Mr. Gioacchino at this time."

My body sat there stunned at what he was saying. Was he really turning me away? Did he really not want to hear about all of Aldo's illegal activity, money laundering, murderers and everything else? How could police officer not want to hear this information? But my gut knew exactly why the police didn't want to hear what I had to say.

I didn't know for sure if this officer was paid off by Aldo, but there were probably dozens of officers in that building who were. It surprised me that they didn't want a chance to make a big headline, though.

"I'm not lying to you. I know where his illegal businesses still are. I know where he buried bodies. I know about the Mayor's daughter overdosing at his house. I have a lot of information that could put him behind bars for the rest of his life," I said emphatically.

"Mr. Stern, do you have proof of any of these things? Proof that Aldo Gioacchino is the one that committed the crimes and not one of the people who worked for him?"

His words sent chills through my body as I replayed all the important events that I had seen Aldo commit. It was true, Aldo always had someone else doing his dirty work for him. He always sent someone else to torture or murder someone. Even thinking back to what happened with Kimberly, Aldo ordered one of his guys to 'take care' of Rocco after the assault.

I shook my head in understanding. I saw what he was getting to. They weren't going to risk going after Aldo unless there was hard, physical proof that Aldo himself had been part of a crime. It was only Aldo that they wanted, and if I couldn't prove his involvement, they didn't want to hear anything I had to say.

"So there is no way you will help?" I asked in dismay.

"We can put out a missing person's report on your girl, would you like us to do that?" "Technically she isn't missing; I mean, I know where she is."

The officer looked less than enthusiastic to be still dealing with me, and I decided it was time for me to think up a new plan. Certainly, the local police weren't going to get involved. The more I thought about it, the more I realized that they probably got paid off with tons of cash by Aldo throughout the years. None of them were going to want to risk their bonus side money that he gave them. "That's all I can offer you for right now?"

"Okay, thanks," I said as I got up to leave.

Officer Reynolds walked me out to the front lobby and then grabbed my arm to say one last thing. "You should just forget about all of this. It's not worth it, you know."

"Abby is worth it," I said as I turned to leave.

Reluctantly, I headed over to Jack's house to talk with him and Isabella and tell them what was going on. Neither of them were going to be happy with me. Jack was certainly not going to like the idea that I had just gone to the police, and Isabella wasn't going to like what I had to tell her about what was going on with Abby and Aldo. But they were the only two I could talk to about everything, and I needed their help. There was no way I was leaving Abby with Aldo, even if I ended up in jail, it would be worth it.

I had made the walk down Fifth Avenue many nights before, but on that specific evening, I paid more attention to the people around. The couples that walked together holding hands looked like they were in a world all of their own. Admittedly, I didn't know if Abby and I would ever have such a relationship, but she was the first woman I had met who actually made me think about that kind of future.

When I arrived at Jack's house, I prepared to tell him everything that had happened with the dinner and Aldo. He was a good friend; we had been closing for so many years, and I had hope that in the end he would understand my choices.

"Hey Theo, what's up?" Jack said as I got to his condo.

"Man, that dinner with Aldo was a trip. He threatened Abby or something and basically said he was keeping her."

"Now, that's some kind of shit. What did you do?"

"I tried to fight for her, but they pulled a gun on me. All over a girl. I can't believe Aldo would go this crazy over a girl."

"Isn't it the same girl that you want to drop your entire life for?" Jack said with a grin.

It was the truth; I knew exactly why Aldo wanted Abby. She had the ability to make him feel good; not just physically good, which I hoped she hadn't been doing. Abby had a way of making me feel like I was a good man, a good person, someone who could do whatever I wanted in my life. The way she could forgive and still care was remarkable. The way she could connect with anyone no matter what walk of life they were in; she had a gift that resonated with me.

"So what's next?" Jack asked as we sat in the living room.

"I went to the police and offered to turn Aldo in and tell them everything I know about him." "You did what?" Jack said as he stood up. "Shit, you are going to get us killed!"

"Stop worrying. The cops wouldn't even talk to me. They don't want to arrest Aldo. They are just as scared of him as we are."

"Theo, I've gone along with this game of yours, and if you want to blow up your own life, that's your business. But you've just made life really dangerous; not just for you but for everyone involved with you. In fact, you might have just gotten Abby killed."

"Jack, I'm trying to get her away from him. He's taking her back to his house and has threatened her with something. I wanted to get Aldo arrested so I could help her, I'm not going to get her killed," I said.

"The police didn't want to deal with you because they are in Aldo's back pocket, right?" "Yeah, exactly. They aren't going to go arrest a guy that is giving them payoffs and shit."

"Then doesn't it make sense that they would go and tell him that you showed up and were trying to have him arrested? That way they look like the good guys, and he'll give them more payoffs."

"Oh shit," I mumbled as I realized what Jack was saying. "They have probably already called him and told him I was there. Fuck, fuck, fuck!"

"I've got an idea. But it means we all need to be okay with dropping everything and running away if it doesn't work," Jack said calmly as he sat down next to me.

"Anything Jack. I need to fix this."

Jack took a minute and wrote down a name on a piece of paper and a phone number. He didn't tell me anything else but just handed me the paper.

"Who is this?" I asked.

"Only call that number if you're ready to give this all up. I'm serious, Theo, like everything would be gone. I won't work for you. The escort business won't exist anymore. Everything," Jack said with an unfamiliar serious expression on his face. "You should get back to your house now. If Aldo is looking for you, I don't want him coming here. Have Mario at your front door for protection tonight."

"You're not going to tell me who this is?" I asked, standing up to leave. "No, I told you the consequences of calling him; that's all I can say."

"Alright, I'll think about it," I said as I left.

It was odd the mystery that Jack had behind calling this guy. Jack and I had always been really open with each other. He had been my right-hand man and more than willing to step up and help out whenever possible. I didn't think we really had any secrets between the two of us, but I figured maybe I didn't know as much as I thought.

There wasn't time to think about things, though, and I certainly didn't want to think about what Aldo might do to Abby when he found out that I had tried to turn him in. I dialed the number as I walked toward my building.

"Hello," the man on the phone answered.

"Hello, is Harrison Stone available?" I asked. "Who is calling?"

The voice on the other end of the phone was calm, yet I could tell he was really interested in knowing who I was. Normally, I wouldn't have been so willing to give my name to a complete stranger, but I didn't have a choice any longer. Time was running out, and I needed someone to help me get Abby out of Aldo's house.

I didn't know what Aldo was going to do with Abby, but I knew he had no problem with killing people, and his wife had already pulled a gun on me and pointed it at Abby's head. I was desperate for help, even if it came from some anonymous person I had called as a last resort.

"Theodore Stern, my friend Jack gave me this number. I have a situation. Who are you? What kind of work do you do? Can you help me?"

"Where are you? I'll be right there," the man said as if he knew exactly who I was and didn't have a problem coming to meet me in the middle of the night.

"Um. I'm on my way home, I could …"

"I'll meet you there in ten minutes," the man interrupted and then hung up the phone.

I felt like a clandestine agent from some sort of spy movie. Who was this guy, and how did he know where I lived? Better yet, how did Jack know this guy? I picked up a pace as I hurried home so I could at least beat him there and talk to Kimberly before he arrived.

"Kim, you need to get your things together and go stay with one of your friends," I said as I hurried into the apartment.

"What? Now?" she asked, bewildered.

"Yes, like now, this second now!" I said as I went into her room and started throwing her things into a bag.

"What's going on?"

"Aldo is going to try and kill me, and probably Abby too; you need to get away from me."

I didn't feel like going into all the details about trying to turn Aldo in or the strange man who was coming to my apartment any minute. I just needed to get Kimberly as far away from me as possible, for her own safety.

Then there was a knock at the door.

"Now, take what you have here and go," I said as I pressed the bag into her hand and pulled her toward the door.

As I opened the door, I pushed Kimberly out and past the strange man that stood in front of me. He wasn't much older than I was, maybe in his early 40s. He was around six feet tall and had on an ominous black suit that matched his jet-black hair. If I hadn't known better, I would have thought he was straight out of one of those spy movies.

"Harrison?" I asked.

"Mr. Stone, if we are going to act we need to act right now. There isn't time to think about anything if you want to get Abigail out of there safely. But you're going to have to agree to cooperate fully and to testify."

"Wait? Who are you? Testify … I went to the police, and they refused to talk to me."

"The FBI has been following Aldo Gioacchino for the last ten years trying to make a case against him.
He's always smart about who he uses and how dirty his hands get. If you'll agree to testify, we believe we can use the testimony in combination with the

evidence we have to put him away for the rest of his life."
"You've been following Aldo?" "Yes."

"So you've been following me too?" "Yes."

"Shit."
"Mr. Stern, we really don't have time for all of this. If my intel is correct, Mr. Gioacchino has already
learned that you went to the police. It's only a matter of time before he sends someone here for you. I also cannot assure the safety of Ms. Tessaro at all at this point."

"Wow, you guys really do see everything. Why haven't you arrested Aldo yet?"

"Originally, our case was centered on you until information gave us some good pieces of evidence that you weren't the biggest fish and we should look more at Mr. Gioacchino. But it was a large amount of cash that you sent home to your family that first tipped us off all those years ago."

"What do you need from me?"

"Everything. You're going to have to give us every dirty detail of your business and your dealings with Aldo. Because we are in a time sensitive situation, I'll take a sworn video statement of the basic information. Then we can work on more detailed information later."

"Will I be arrested?'

"It's possible if your information is good enough that we will be able to work out a deal, but I can't guarantee it since we won't have time to verify the information. I'll be honest with you, Mr. Stern, you're going to have to do this with the understanding that you might end up with charges and going to jail."

I needed his help, and he was the only person in the world that was willing to go up against Aldo. There wasn't anything for me to think about. I was going to be murdered and so was Abby if I didn't make the deal. Life in prison sounded like a much better life than getting murdered.

"I understand," I said although I certainly didn't fully understand what was going on.

"Okay," he said as he dialed a number on his phone. "Mr. Stern is on board, we are a go."

Chapter 17

ABBY

"He did what!" Aldo screamed into his phone as I came out of the bathroom. "I'll fucking kill him."

I looked over toward Nicole, and the concerned expression on her face told me that she also had no idea what Aldo was talking about. But Nicole had been married long enough to the man that she didn't bother to ask him at all. I, on the other hand, couldn't stand not knowing.

"What's going on? Anything I can help with?" I asked as I tried to make myself useful. "What is wrong with you? Why do you look disgusting," Aldo yelled at me.

"Aldo, she was in the bathroom vomiting, give the poor girl a break," Nicole interjected. "Take her to her room; I don't want to see her," Aldo said with a look of disgust.

I hadn't quite seen a look like that on Aldo toward me before, and I felt like it had something to do with whatever was going on with his phone call. My stomach churned for real as Nicole walked me to the room they wanted me to stay in. Everything felt like it was falling apart. In the span of only a few hours, I had gone from thinking that life was great, to being scared for my own life.

Sometimes, I had to wonder what was going on in my head and why I made the decisions I did. As I sat on the well-adorned bed and Nicole shut the door to leave me there, I felt real fear for what was going to happen next. Aldo hadn't actually liked me, it was obvious by how quickly he had turned against me as soon as something went wrong. I shouldn't have agreed to go out with Aldo in the first place. That very first day when I was with Theo and Aldo had made me the offer of ten thousand dollars. It was that moment that I regretted the most.

Even when I sent the money home to my sisters, I knew that it was money that I shouldn't have earned the way I did. Sure, I talked myself into it and made myself believe that everything was fine, but deep down I felt like shit taking Aldo's money. It felt like a snake was circling around me, and I was trying to ignore the fact that he could kill me at any moment. The horrible part of it all was that I knew better. I
wasn't stupid, I had been in New York for years. I knew better than to get involved in the kind of shit that I had gotten myself into. But the money had blinded me.

Even Theo was the kind of guy that I should have avoided when I started seeing him throwing his money around on the trip to Vegas. I knew better than to trust a guy who would spend that kind of money on a woman he hardly knew. But I was starting to have feelings for Theo that I hadn't had before, and it was too hard for me to just walk away from him.

But as I sat there on the bed, locked in a room at Aldo's house, I finally realized that money really
couldn't buy you any sort of happiness. Just looking at Aldo and his wife, you could see that it didn't matter how much money they had, it was never enough, and they weren't happy. At that moment, I decided I needed to be with my sisters. The years of me hiding from the reality of life had to end. I was a jerk for leaving them and never going back for them. Sending money to them wasn't at all like being there to support them. They were my sisters and I loved them, and I obviously wasn't going to make it big in New York; so I needed to go home to them. That was if I could get myself out of the situation I had gotten into.

"I should just fucking kill her!" I heard Aldo scream as he threw something in the living room.

I could hear that Nicole was talking to him softly, but I couldn't make out what she was saying. Whatever was going on was pretty huge and it had pissed him off enough that he was talking about killing me. I was scared. More scared than I could ever remember feeling, and I had been in some pretty shady situations over the years. Aldo was the kind of guy who could kill anyone he wanted; I was more sure of that now than I had been when Theo had talked about him. If only I could figure out why he was so damn angry, maybe there would have been a way to calm him down.

But my ways of manipulating people in my favor only worked so well and only worked when I knew what was going on. At that moment, I had no idea what was going on or why Aldo was so damn angry with me.

I looked out the window to see if there was any way to escape the room they had put me in, but we were up in a high-rise and there were no balconies. Even if I could have opened the window, it surely would have been the death of me if I had jumped. No, I decided I was just going to have to wait and hope that Nicole could calm her husband down. Or hope that whatever had pissed him off so much would calm him down.

I tried to listen at the door to hear what was going on, but I couldn't hear anything. There was no more screaming and no more throwing things around. It was either a good sign or a really bad one, and I decided to sit in the corner and see if I could reach Theo.

When I pulled my phone out, I saw that Theo had tried to call me. It was far too dangerous for me to be on the telephone at all, and I certainly couldn't call him back. I text him again.

"Aldo says he's going to kill me. Please, if there is anything you can do. Help me," I sent to him.

Instantly, I could see that he had read the message and was responding. I waited in anticipation for his message to appear in return. I didn't know Theo much better than I knew Aldo, but there was one thing I knew for sure; Theo wouldn't hurt me. He cared about me, and I knew it in my soul. Whatever else happened before or after that moment, I knew that Theo would try and help me.

"Coming there now, hide if you can," Theo responded. "Can't text anymore. Do whatever you have to. I'm coming for you."

I felt relieved when I read his message, although logically, I knew I was still in a lot of danger. It wouldn't take Aldo very long to kill me if that was really what he wanted to do. Certainly, one bullet to my brain would only take a few seconds once he got into the room I was in. I decided I had to start putting all the furniture in front of the door. Anything necessary so I could slow down the process.

As soon as I had pushed the nightstand in front of the door, I heard the jiggling of the handle. The fear inside of me was so much that I felt like my whole body go cold and was unable to move as I stared at the door handle and waited for my killer to force himself into my room.

"It's me," I heard Nicole say.

Although Nicole had been the one who held the gun up to my head in the restaurant, I didn't feel like she actually wanted to hurt me. The move had seemed more like something she was doing to impress her husband and to scare Theo. She was the only person I could hope to help me, so I pushed the nightstand out of the way and let her in.

"Why does he want to kill me?" I asked as Nicole came into the room and closed the door.

"It's Theo, he went to the police and tried to turn Aldo in. The police wouldn't deal with him, so hopefully, everything is fine. But Aldo doesn't want to deal with you anymore. I've convinced him to give you to Briggs. I know it's not ideal. I'm sorry."

"What? Briggs? Oh, my God," I said as tears started down my face.

There weren't many times in my life where I had actually felt hopeless. Usually, I felt like if I worked hard enough, I could figure a solution out. But at that moment, I felt everything being pulled from me and didn't have the ability to think clearly. I wasn't in charge any longer, and that was a place I wasn't used to being in.

Being in charge was how I made myself feel better. I could make a man love me, and I could drop him just as quickly when I didn't need anything from him any longer. Of course, I hated that I hurt people, but I was much better at hurting others than I was at letting myself get hurt.

"Listen to me, Abigail. Briggs is just like any other man. You hear me? I know you can deal with him."

The way Nicole looked at me made me see her in a whole different light than I had seen here before. It was like she knew I had been manipulating men all along, even her husband. She had a look of knowing in her eyes as she held onto my arms and shook me back to reality.

Women and I didn't get along much. Isabella had been my only true female friend since I had arrived in New York. But Nicole was like me; I saw it in her eyes and felt it in her hands as they held onto my arms. She wanted to help me, and I needed to listen to her.

It is weird, how in moments of sheer panic, you can hone in your own body's ability to function. Suddenly, I felt in control and more able to handle the situation. Knowing that there was at least one other human being that was with me and on my side made everything seem much less hopeless.

"What should I do?" I asked urgently.

"Your sick thing is good. Use that again, but can you make yourself actually vomit?" she asked.

There was no time for games; I couldn't pretend not to understand what she was talking about. Surely, she already knew that I had pretended to be ill so I wouldn't have to sleep with her or with Aldo. At that moment, I felt an alliance with her that was so unusual, yet so pure.

Whatever Nicole had been through with Aldo had put her in a position where she wanted to help me. Sure, it was probably purely because she felt they might be arrested, and she wanted it to look good that she had made some sort of effort. Or maybe she really did have a sister alliance with me and wanted to help me, but it didn't really matter to me at that moment. She was all I had.

"Yes, I can."

"Then do that. I'm going to have to be on Aldo's side. But if something happens, and there are police, please get me out," she said with a longing in her eyes. "I was like you once. I thought I could handle this life. But if I can get out, make it happen for me."

"I will do anything I can," I said, and I meant it.

Nicole didn't have to come into that room and warn me about what was going on. She didn't have to give me that small moment of hope. So if it came to something down the road where I could offer her help, I would do my best to make sure I helped.

Women needed to stick together, at least, the ones who understood my way of thinking and looking at the world. I was willing to bet that Nicole hadn't gotten to the place she was in life without living a little outside of the norm.

I was willing to bet that she was much more like me than many of the women in the world. Aldo probably had sucked her into his life, just like he had sucked me in. She put on a strong persona and pretended to be in control as a way of protecting herself. I knew what that was like very much.

"Thanks," she said as she hugged me and then left the room.

I stood there in total awe as I tried to soak in what had just happened and what was about to happen. I could only hope that whoever Theo was coming with was indeed the police and they were going to be there before Briggs came for me. The horror stories that Briggs himself had told of what he liked to do to women was enough to make my blood go cold. I really didn't know if I could fend off a man like that.

Quickly I looked around the room for anything that I could use as a weapon and hide in my bag. The room was pretty much emptied out with only the basic furnishing still around, but I remembered watching a crime drama where the woman had stolen a spring from under a bed and killed her captor with it. Certainly, I hoped I wouldn't have to kill anyone, but I laid down and looked under the bed frame to see if there were springs there that I could use.

Sure enough, there were long nine-inch springs under the bed. I had to pull with all my strength to get one of them free, and as I did, it collapsed on my finger and sliced it opened. The cut was big and the blood started dripping all over, so I held the finger against my chest in an effort to get the bleeding to stop.

There was a knock at the front door, and I instantly felt like I was going to pass out. It was either Theo with whoever he was coming to the house with or it was Briggs, coming to get me. I slid down into the corner of the bedroom and waited to see who it was.

The talking in the living room made me instantly think that it was Briggs and not whoever Theo had
planned to come to the apartment with. Certainly, Aldo wasn't going to talk with Theo when he arrived.

As the footsteps toward my room got louder, I felt myself getting dizzier and dizzier. I could hardly breathe from anticipation and fear as the doorknob to my room opened, and I saw Briggs standing there.

"She's all yours," I heard Aldo's voice say from behind him.

Briggs shut the door and locked it behind him. He had a disgusting look on his face and a smile that spanned across his crooked teeth. I wanted to scream but was afraid to. I wanted to run but knew there was no way out of that room. I was stuck, and there wasn't a damn thing I could do about it.

"Now this is going to be fun," Briggs said as he yanked me up from the ground and threw me onto the bed.

"Please, I'm sick. Please, let's go back to your place. I promise to do whatever you want," I pleaded with him.

"You seem to forget my dear. I don't like to make my women happy. I like to make them scream," he said as his fist hauled off and hit me across the jaw.

For a moment, I thought I was going to be alright, but then I felt the room go dark. The pain hurt in a throbbing and pounding sort of way as I opened my eyes and tried to get my bearings to what was going on. I expected that Briggs would have been on top of me or assaulting me in some way, but instead, he was just sitting in a chair watching me.

The blood from my finger had covered the sheets, and my lip was dripping blood as well. But I didn't scream. I knew better than to give him that satisfaction. If there was anything I could do to prevent it, I wasn't going to scream for that bastard. I wasn't going to give him the pleasure.

There was a loud bang that sounded like it was coming from the front door, and Briggs jumped up to go see what was going on. He opened the door and then quickly shut it again and locked it. I had also jumped up by this point and moved back to the corner of the room where I slid down to the ground and watched as Briggs started piling things up in front of the door. Whoever had come through that front door had scared Briggs enough that he no longer cared about assaulting me, and instead, was hiding in the room with me.

"What's going on?" I asked as we heard Aldo screaming.

"I'm going to kill you bitch. You aren't going to testify against me," Aldo screamed at Nicole.

Briggs ran into the bathroom and shut the door, leaving me alone in the bedroom as the gunshots continued. I stayed low on the ground in the corner and just hoped that none of them would fly through a wall and hit me.

I heard Nicole screaming for help, and I don't know what came over me but I jumped up and opened the door. There I was face to face with Aldo. He had Nicole in front of him and was holding her hair in a fist with a gun in his other hand as he looked toward the front door. Something came over me at that moment, and I looked at Nicole and knew what I had to do.

Chapter 18

THEO

Agent Stone had tried to tell me I couldn't go with him to the raid on Aldo's house. But at some point, he finally gave in and allowed me to stay downstairs. I wasn't just going to stay at my apartment while they took Aldo down, not after what he had put me through. I wanted him to know that I was the one who had put him in jail. I wanted him to understand that I wasn't just some jerk kid that needed him to lead him for the rest of his life.

Sure, I was willing to own up to the mistakes I had made so far in my life. If that meant I had to do jail time, then I was going to do it. But I didn't have to let Aldo control me at all. Life was too short to keep living his dreams. I had my own dreams, and I didn't care any longer if there was money in my hands while I went after those dreams.

"I swear to God you need to stay here; if you leave this damn vehicle, I will shoot you myself," Agent Stone said to me as we pulled up to Aldo's building.

"Go, go, go," came the call over the radio in his SUV while I waited.

I couldn't hear everything that was going on but only the radio communication that went on among all the federal agents that were involved. It was like listening to a crime show and trying to figure out what was happening without being able to see it.

Nothing in my life made any sense at that moment without Abby. All I knew was that these agents needed to get her out of that house, and I wasn't going to be okay until that happened. I could feel my heart pounding in my chest with the anticipation of what was going on, and I even said a little prayer in hopes that Abby was going to be released without Aldo hurting her.

I knew Aldo well enough to know that he would panic as soon as the police arrived. He would try to kill Abby and maybe even his own wife if he thought they would turn against him when he got arrested.
Although Aldo had the ability of being extremely charming, he was a deadly

guy who would only look out for himself when things got messy.

As I sat in the SUV and tried to be patient and wait for the whole thing to be over, I got a horrible pit in my stomach. It wasn't something I could just forget about. Abby was in danger, and I didn't want to just sit in a damn vehicle and hope that someone else would save her.

"Shots fired, shots fired," a man said over the radio.

"Man down, believed to be suspect. Man down," another voice said.

"I hear a woman screaming from the back room; I'm going to check it out," a third voice that sounded like Agent Stone said.

There was silence and then someone pressed their button to open up the communication channel and I could hear a woman screaming. The scream was so soul wrenching that I jumped out of the vehicle and made my way into the building. It was Abby, and I knew it; I had to get to her. I had to do whatever I could to save her.

They had turned off all the elevators for their raid of Aldo's place, so I had to use the stairs to get up to his floor. I couldn't stop myself as I flew up the stairs two and three steps at a time. I didn't' get tired and couldn't imagine stopping for anything. There was only one thing on my mind, and that was getting to Abby.

In my heart, I knew that Aldo would try to kill her so she couldn't testify against him. I knew he was smart enough not to leave witnesses alive. Even if he knew I had turned him in, he wasn't about to leave Abby alive to agree with my story. My stomach felt like it was being ripped in half as I got to the top of the stairs and heard the deafening woman's scream.

When I opened the stairwell, two men quickly pointed their guns at me and forced me down to the ground. One of them had their knee on my back and was screaming at me before I could even get a word out of my mouth.

I had been arrested before. But I knew, from working with Aldo, that most of the time it was the suspect who gave the officers the information they needed to make a case. Over the years, all the times I had been arrested were dismissed after I refused to talk to them at all.

But this moment was different; I couldn't hold back and began desperately trying to explain who I was and why I was there. I didn't have time for them to arrest or detain me; I needed to get to Abby.

"My girlfriend is in there," I yelled at them. "Let me see her," I begged.

There were no more gunshots going off, but there was plenty of commotion and that woman's voice still screaming in the background. The screaming was much calmer now, though, and I suspected it wasn't Abby any longer. For some reason, I felt like I knew what Abby's scream would sound like. It was weird, and totally not based on any facts, but my gut at that moment told me that the screaming belonged to someone else.

"Let him up," I heard a man say. "So, I can shoot him."

I looked up to see Agent Stone standing over me. He grabbed me by the arm and pulled me into the living room where I saw Aldo's bodyguard dead on the ground. The room was destroyed, and I looked around to see where the woman was who had been screaming.

The woman's screams had died down and were now cries and a sort of wailing, and they were coming from the back room. It still made my heart ache to hear a woman crying like that, and I was desperate to make sure it wasn't Abby.

Despite the business I was in, I loved women. Many people thought it was the other way around, and that I couldn't possibly like women if I ran an escort business. But I did love them. I wanted them to have the money and success they dreamed of and knew how to help them get it. Of course, I also did my best to ensure their safety as much as possible. Up until recently, I had strictly researched anyone who wanted to date one of my girls. But as the business had grown, my ability to research everyone had declined.

What happened to Kimberly had been an eye-opening event for me and not something I took lightly. I certainly wouldn't have killed the guy like Aldo did. But I made sure he understood that that sort of violence against my women wasn't allowed.

"I really should shoot you," Agent Stone said. "But I'll leave these two to deal with you for now."

He opened the door to a back room where I saw Nicole and Abby huddled together and covered in blood. Nicole was the one crying and seemed to be covered from head to toe in blood. Her hands were shaking, and Abby had her arms wrapped around her.

"Are medics on the way?" I asked Agent Stone as he walked away.

"No need for medics, everyone's dead. But yeah, we will take the ladies in to get checked out." "Are you okay?" I said to Abby as I stood in the doorway and looked down at her.

She was remarkably calm as she held Nicole in her arms. It was clear that Nicole had been the one who was screaming but certainly not clear what had made her scream so much.

"We are okay," Abby said calmly. "Briggs is in the bathroom hiding, though, get an officer in here to arrest him."

Abby nodded toward a door near her, and I went to grab one of the agents. They quickly broke the door down and dragged Briggs out of the bathroom. He was crying like a little boy and shaking. It struck me as funny that such a rotten man had such a big fear of being arrested.

A medic team came in and pushed me out of the way as they went right to Nicole and Abby. Although Abby's hands were covered in blood, Nicole's whole body had it on her. The team pulled her away from Abby and quickly started to look her over.

"I'm alright," Abby said as one of the medics talked to her. "Take care of Nicole, I'm alright." "I'm sorry," I mouthed to Abby from the doorway as she dealt with the medics.

There wasn't anything else I could say at that moment, and I couldn't get close enough to actually talk to her. I stood in the doorway and peeked down toward the other back room where all the officers kept coming in and out of.

My curiosity got the best of me, and I took a few steps down the hallway and saw Aldo laying on the ground with what looked like a bed spring right through his eye. There also appeared to be a gun only a few feet away from his hand, and he had multiple gunshot wounds to his chest.

When I looked back at Abby, she just shrugged her shoulders at me and then mouthed something that I wasn't sure I understood. She had a smirk on her face that threw me off and didn't seem to fit the moment at all, and I swore she said something about lemonade.

"I made lemonade," Abby said.

"Lemonade?" I asked louder so she could hear me.

"Remember, life isn't about the lemons, it's about the lemonade you make," she said with a sly grin, loud enough that I could hear her.

I did remember that saying, and it seemed odd to me that she would bring it up at a time like this. My gut told me that Abby might have been the real one who had killed Aldo but that Nicole was taking the rap for it. On the other hand, Nicole was the one covered in blood, so who was going to argue with the idea that she had done it.

As I looked at the two women, though, I noticed that Nicole's hands weren't covered in blood at all. Her body had it all over, but her hands were clean. My mind thought through all the possibilities of what had gone on when Abby and Nicole were left with Aldo. I couldn't know for sure, but my guess was that one of those two had murdered him.

"Ma'am, did you stab your husband with the spring?" an agent asked Nicole.

She was still shaking and crying, but she looked up at the officer and calmed down just enough to answer him. Nicole had always struck me as a woman who knew exactly how to get what she wanted from someone. She wouldn't have lasted as long as she did with Aldo if she wasn't like that.

I did feel bad for her, though; the whole life she had built was gone and she was a lawyer who would probably never work again in her life. Or at least, not work with normal clients again; it was highly likely that other underground clients were going to want to be involved with her.

"He had a gun to my head and was going to kill me," she said calmly.

She was good, Nicole knew exactly what she needed to say in order to say she had killed Aldo in self-defense. Plus, who knew if it was really her who had killed him or not. Perhaps it had been the federal agents who had delivered the final blow.

All in all, I suspected that Nicole was going to end up just fine. Aldo had dozens of bank accounts in other countries, and I was positive that Nicole knew how to get access to them. With Aldo out of the way, she was going to be free and clear to spend the rest of his money however she wanted.

Of course, the government was going to take all his assets and money that was left in the United States. But Aldo was a smart man, and Nicole an extremely smart woman. They had millions in assets located throughout the globe, and as soon as things settled down, I was sure she would disappear and live a life she had dreamed of.

"We will need to ask you some more questions after you get medically cleared," the agent said and then went over to Abby.

"Ma'am, did you see what happened?"

"Aldo was dragging her down the hallway and saying he couldn't have any witnesses. I just heard screaming, and then she stabbed him and I pulled her into the room and locked the door to protect us. There was a lot of commotion; I'm sorry that's all I know."

I knew Abby was lying. I didn't know her well enough to say it for sure, but something in my gut told me that what she was saying was to protect Nicole. I certainly wasn't going to say a word and instead just stood by and watched as the agent asked his questions and then left the room.

"I think I'm going to be sick," Abby said.

Her hands were shaking, and she looked really pale; I couldn't wait any longer and pushed my way past the medics and grabbed a hold of her. She had a large gash in her finger, which I put pressure on. But I suspected her adrenaline was dying off a bit, and her body was reacting to the changes.

"Did you say you made lemonade?" I asked. "Yep," she said as she looked at

me.

I really thought she was going a little bit crazy from the emotions of everything. We both sort of laughed a strangled and stressed out laugh as we looked into each other's eyes. All I knew for sure was that Abby was alright, and I was so grateful for that.

"I don't know; it seems like an odd time for lemonade," I laughed back.

"Can you call my sisters?" Abby asked. "Bring them out here, I need to see them."

"I'll get it done. I do have to go talk to this agent and try to avoid jail first," I said as I saw Agent Stone standing in the doorway.

"No big deal, though, right?" Abby said with a smile.

"I got this," I said without a single shred of confidence in the words I spoke.

It was entirely possible that I would go and talk to the federal agents and they were going to throw me in jail for the rest of my life. They had not promised me any kind of immunity, and I had not required it to help them. All I had wanted was for Abby to be safe, and I was so excited to be there with her and know that she was.

"Good, because my feet are killing me, and I need a massage." Abby laughed as she kicked off her new Steve Madden hi-heels.

Everyone around us looked at us like we were crazy, but Abby and I both smiled at the memory of the first time we met and I lost her damn shoes.

Epilogue

"Samantha, you are going to have to actually carry some of your own things up these stairs, we aren't going to do it all for you," I yelled at my sister as I tried to get her to help with the boxes of things we were bringing to her dorm room.

"I just did my nails, Abby, you can't expect me to mess them up over some boxes. Plus, you and Bailey are much stronger than I am," she said with a childish grin.

"It's amazing to me how she can get out of doing absolutely any work,"

Bailey said. "I don't actually mind," I said as we made it to the third floor.

"I'm pretty sure they invented these horrible pieces of furniture as some sort of torture device," Theo said as we got to the dorm room. "There aren't even enough screws to hold this damn thing together."

"Do you need this?" Bailey asked as she handed Theo a small pack of screws that was sitting by the doorway.

"God Damnit!"

It was so good to have my sisters in New York and near me. I couldn't believe we had taken so long to make the decision to have them just come out and have us all be together. Of course, our parents' business and home ended up getting auctioned off by the bank. But Bailey and Samantha had saved the ten thousand dollars I sent them and used it to pack up all their things and bought a car to drive out to New York.

Theo's assets were frozen, and he didn't have access to most of his money while he went through court proceedings for his case. The judge said he was lucky he wasn't in jail for the rest of his life. But I secretly thought the judge liked Theo. One year of house arrest in Theo's plush condo wasn't really something I considered as a punishment. Plus, the judge ruled that Theo could keep his restaurant and his gym.

I stopped working at the dance club and instead took up classes to get my personal trainers' certificate and Sunrise, the manager of Theo's gym, had turned out to be one of my best friends over the previous few months.

"Aren't we supposed to be at dinner with Jack and Isabella soon?" I asked Theo as I looked at the pile of wood that was supposed to be a bunk bed.

"You're going to have to go without me, this bed is like a puzzle only an idiot savant could answer." "Let me take a look at it," Scott said as he sat down.

"I'm an idiot savant."

"A hot idiot savant," Bailey whispered in my ear.

"Shhh, he's Theo's employee. Don't be rude," I whispered back.

"I said he's hot. It's not like I mentioned that he was missing a leg."

"Jesus Bailey, shut up," I said, embarrassed that Scott might have heard her.

"Do you want to touch it?" Scott said with a smile as he looked at Bailey.

"Mmm, yeah, I want to touch it," Bailey said as she sat down next to Scott and touched his metal prosthetic leg.

"I think we are witnessing a budding romance," Theo said as he stood up and came over to me.

"Do you guys mind if we leave? We are going to be late for dinner," I said, looking at Samantha and Bailey.

Samantha was on her cell phone texting someone and barely looked up at me, and Bailey was enthralled with Scott and didn't seem to notice we were even in the room. The moment was so surreal and yet so happy. I felt like life was finally going well for all of us. We couldn't have planned a single moment of it and certainly couldn't have expected we would end up where we had, but life was pretty damn good.

"It's alright guys, I've got this," Scott said as he turned toward us. "I'll make sure Bailey gets back over to your place when we are done."

"Thanks," Theo said as he grabbed my hand and pulled me out of the dorm room.

"Wait, he's going to bring her home? What do you know about this guy? I don't know," I said, following behind Theo.

"She's a big girl, let her flirt a little," Theo said as he stopped and pulled me up next to him. "Maybe we will actually have the apartment to ourselves for a little bit this afternoon."

His lips moved to mine, and I instantly felt the stress of moving Samantha just melt away. Theo did that for me, he had done it from the moment I met him and every second we were together since then.

"What about lunch with Isabella and Jack?" I said as I saw the look of desire in Theo's eyes.

"Isabella's pregnant, you know they will already have eaten by the time we get all the way to the restaurant. Let's just call and cancel. We can go to lunch another day."

Theo was right; Isabella was three months pregnant and couldn't stop eating for more than an hour or so. It was so great to see her happy and still with Jack. I never would have thought they would have lasted as long as they had, but something just clicked for them, and they were happy.

That's all any of us wanted really ... happiness. Well, and shoes, of course.

THE END

Printed in Great Britain
by Amazon